The Search for Noah

"Where is he?" Delphine demanded to know, gazing about for anything resembling a hospital.

"There are six regimental hospitals," Dr. Hutchings said. "Those three tents are one of them."

"We go there." Delphine hiked her shortened skirts.

"Oh no, Miss Duval." The doctor put out a hand to bar her way—never a good idea. "No women—ladies—are allowed in the hospital tents. It's entirely for your own good. The men are in their underwear, and there are no blankets and . . ." Dr. Hutchings was getting right down to the end of his rope.

Delphine had drawn up to her almost five feet without the heeled slippers. She glanced back at me, and her veiled eyes sparked their dark fire. "This girl's brother is in that tent. Is it so?"

Dr. Hutchings admitted it was.

"You are not an officer to command me. And me, I am not a soldier." She pointed herself out with a gloved finger. "And if I was, I wouldn't be soldiering on this side. Get the quilt," she said to me.

The doctor was this close to wringing his hands. "Truly, Miss Pruitt," he said as we bore down on the tent flap, "I can't permit—" But it would have taken five or six men his size to keep us out. I wanted my brother.

BOOKS BY RICHARD PECK

Amanda/Miranda

Are You in the House Alone?

The Dreadful Future of Blossom Culp

Dreamland Lake

Fair Weather

Father Figure

The Ghost Belonged to Me

Ghosts I Have Been

Invitations to the World

A Long Way from Chicago

Lost in Cyberspace

Past Perfect, Present Tense

The River Between Us

Strays Like Us

The Teacher's Funeral: A Comedy in Three Parts

A Year Down Yonder

RICHARD PECK

The River Between Us

PUFFIN BOOKS

PUFFIN BOOKS
Published by the Penguin Group
Penguin Young Readers Group, 345 Hudson Street, New York, New York 10014, U.S.A.
Penguin Group (Canada), 10 Alcorn Avenue, Toronto,
Ontario, Canada M4V 3B2 (a division of Pearson Penguin Canada Inc.)
Penguin Books Ltd, 80 Strand, London WC2R 0RL, England
Penguin Ireland, 25 St Stephen's Green, Dublin 2, Ireland (a division of Penguin Books Ltd)
Penguin Group (Australia), 250 Camberwell Road, Camberwell, Victoria 3124,
Australia (a division of Pearson Australia Group Pty Ltd)
Penguin Books India Pvt Ltd, 11 Community Centre,
Panchsheel Park, New Delhi - 110 017, India
Penguin Group (NZ), Cnr Airborne and Rosedale Roads, Albany, Auckland,
New Zealand (a division of Pearson New Zealand Ltd)
Penguin Books (South Africa) (Pty) Ltd, 24 Sturdee Avenue,
Rosebank, Johannesburg 2196, South Africa

Registered Offices: Penguin Books Ltd, 80 Strand, London WC2R 0RL, England

First published in the United States of America by Dial Books,
a division of Penguin Young Readers Group, 2003
Published by Puffin, a division of Penguin Young Readers Group, 2005

27 29 30 28 26

THE LIBRARY OF CONGRESS HAS CATALOGED THE DIAL EDITION AS FOLLOWS:
Peck, Richard, date.
The river between us / Richard Peck.
p. cm.
Summary: During the early years of the Civil War, the Pruitt family takes in
two mysterious young ladies who have fled New Orleans to come north to Illinois.
ISBN 0-8037-2735-6
1. United States—History—Civil War, 1861–1865—Juvenile fiction.
[1. United States—History—Civil War, 1861–1865—Fiction. 2. Racially mixed people—Fiction.
3. Family life—Illinois—Fiction. 4. Race relations—Fiction.
5. New Orleans (La.)—Social life and customs—19th century—Fiction.
6. Illinois—History—1778–1865—Fiction.] I. Title.
PZ7.P338 Ri 2003
[Fic]—dc21 2002034815

Puffin Books ISBN 0-14-240310-5

This book is dedicated in long friendship to
Marilyn and Phil Smith

The River Between Us

The Model T Ford Touring Car

1916

Chapter One

To me, the best part was that we'd make the trip by car. When I say car, I mean a Ford, of course, a Model T touring car, and they don't make them like that anymore. In those days it was a big thing to drive a car out of town, let alone a hundred miles each way of Southern Illinois dirt road. I thought the journey itself was going to be the adventure.

My dad made house calls in the Ford. He was a very well-thought-of doctor in the St. Louis of that time. A tall man with black curly hair parted in the middle and steel-rimmed spectacles gripping the bridge of his nose. He wore high celluloid collars, and I never saw him without a necktie.

I thought he carried all the wisdom of the world in the black bag that traveled to house calls with him on the front seat of the Ford. With the same silent skill that he used to set a bone, he could patch a tire.

Apparently, my dad had been young once, but I couldn't picture it. Even at the age of fifteen I knew but little about who he was and where he'd come from. And so I knew but little about myself.

My dad was what they called a self-made man. Though he'd succeeded in St. Louis, he'd come from a little town called Grand Tower on the other side of the Mississippi River down low in Illinois.

All I knew of Dad's people was that they'd lived through the Civil War. Imagine an age when there were still people around who'd seen U. S. Grant with their own eyes, and men who'd voted for Lincoln. People you could reach out and touch.

My dad's father, the first Dr. William Hutchings, had been a doctor in the Union Army. My grandmother and grandfather Hutchings still lived in what Dad called the homeplace, down in Grand Tower, that wide spot in the road.

I couldn't remember visiting them before. My mother was very standoffish about my dad's side of the family. She was a St. Louis girl, and we boys were named for her side of the family. I was Howard Leland Hutchings. My little brothers, twins, were Raymond and Earl. At the age of five, they were too young to figure much in this story, but they came along on the trip too.

Dad worked a six-and-a-half-day week. It was a great occasion when he found an afternoon to take me to a Browns game. That was before the Browns forsook St. Louis to be the Baltimore Orioles.

But now he had announced that we were going to visit his folks—motoring there and back in the Ford. It was the summer of 1916, and war was raging across Europe, the Great War. Dad said it was just a question of time before America got in it. In wartime there'd be restrictions on travel, and so it was now or never.

The next thing I remember is the morning we left, like the dawn of creation. It was a July day breathless with St. Louis heat and the thrill of the open road unwinding before us. Our preparations had taken days. We'd been through the toolbox time and again. We'd filled as many cans of gasoline as we could strap to the running boards. Dad had personally filed down the points on the spark plugs. I hadn't slept a wink in two nights, and now the moment of leaving was upon us.

Mother wasn't going and didn't want us to go. And I didn't know why. I remember her up on the porch and the Ford there in the middle of Maryland Avenue. Dad and I wore dusters and caps with goggles. One of the extra features of our Ford was a windshield. But it was always laid flat across the hood for city driving. The Ford was a touring car, which meant it had a canvas pull-up roof in case of rain, or for when you spent a night on the road.

You had to crank the car a good ten minutes to get it going, and Dad left that part to me. The knack for starting a Ford was to jack up a rear wheel. He got the little boys settled on the rear seat, but they kept spilling out of the car, running back to the house for something they'd forgotten. I wondered if we'd ever get away.

But at last the engine caught and turned over. The Ford coughed twice and came to life. Dad broke a fresh egg into the radiator so that it would hard-boil and seal the leaks. The boys were more or less settled. Dad let out the brake and fiddled with the gas lever. We'd already aroused the neighborhood. Now we were off in a volley of sharp reports from the tailpipe. And Mother was turning back to the house.

I ought to have kept a journal of the trip, but that's not the way of a fifteen-year-old boy. I remember we were hardly over on the Illinois side before Earl learned he was subject to car sickness and Raymond was hit with a great wave of homesickness. Dad had something in his black bag for Earl. He cured Raymond by saying it wasn't too late to take him back home and leave him behind.

Dad's plan was to keep the Mississippi River on our right side and try to be in the vicinity of Chester, Illinois, by nightfall. We made good time on dry roads south from Dupo and didn't have our first flat until very near Waterloo.

In all, we did pretty well with only four flats that day, one in each tire. But it seemed like the Ford was on a jack more than it was on the road. We pumped the tires up by hand. The last sign we saw for free air was outside Columbia.

The little boys needed a steady flow of water from the bottles we'd brought. This made for endless stops at the side of the road. This was a strictly men-only expedition, so we occasionally all four stood in a row over a ditch when the road was empty both directions. An hour of driving would pass before we'd see another car.

We'd pull up by open pasture and drop a ruler into the tank to gauge the gas level. The tank was set in right under the front seats, so it was like riding a bomb, though I never heard of one going off. On our stops, the boys could run wild in the field, wrestling and tussling and mauling each other like puppies. I couldn't remember being that age.

While we were watching them, Dad said, "Twins run in families and tend to skip a generation."

"Was your dad a twin?"

"My mother and her brother are twins. You'll meet Noah. They all live together in the homeplace. My dad and mother and my aunt and uncle. People lived however they could in years past, sharing out what they had. Seemed like most of my dad's patients paid him in fish out of the river and vegetables out of their gardens. A doctor doesn't get rich in Grand Tower."

"So you had four parents," I said.

"In a manner of speaking, I did." Dad watched the boys.

"It wasn't a bad way to grow up. They taught me how to make do, and to keep my private business private. Pretty good lessons."

Down around Red Bud the ruts were deeper, and there was more standing water. We were getting farther into Southern Illinois, the territory they call Egypt for some reason. The farms were hardscrabble yellow clay. They plowed around trees growing clumped in the middles of fields. Two or three hills were so steep that we had to turn the Ford around and go up in reverse. So when the sun was getting down in the west, it was time to call it a day.

Two things my dad mistrusted: water from an unfamiliar well and all hotel rooms on the Illinois side of the river. He could give you a short and sweet scientific description of the common bedbug that made you happy to spend the night on the same car seat you'd bounced along on all day.

We pulled off the road just at dusk and built a little campfire. The boys found sticks to roast wienies on. Now we were early explorers, of the Lewis and Clark party, sitting cross-legged around the wilderness fire. Dad sat just out of the glow on the running board. With any luck, we'd be in Grand Tower tomorrow night by this time.

He must have wondered what the place would look like to us city boys who until today had thought the whole world was paved.

"There never was a lot to Grand Tower," he said, "though it showed some progress after the war. When I was a boy, they had a saddle factory, a cigar plant, a gunsmith shop or two, a brick works. Enos Walker started a sawmill that peeled logs and made strips for splint baskets. My uncle Noah worked there for years."

The little boys' eyes were glazing over. "But it's not much more than a ghost town now," Dad remarked.

This alerted the boys. They looked around with big eyes. The trees were black with night, and now they noticed where they were. "A ghost town isn't quite the same thing as a ghost," Dad said. But seeing he had their full attention, he added, "Of course, every little old town had a haunt or two."

From back in the trees came the rushing of some night bird's wings. The rusty creak of a turning windpump sounded across the darkness.

"There's a hill over the town called the Devil's Backbone," Dad said.

Ghosts and now the devil. He had us in the palm of his hand.

"The house where I grew up straddles the Backbone about halfway along. Now a road runs between the Backbone and the river. A ghost or something very like it has been seen crossing that road on dark nights like this."

I suspected Dad was playing up the story for us, but it worked on me like a charm. The boys were about in each other's laps.

"It's a woman," Dad said, "in old-time skirts with gray hair streaming down her back. She'll dart out in the road, running hard, making for the river, where she seems to throw herself in. It's been reported for years. Any number of horses have shied, and buggies turned over. There are people who won't go down that road after dark."

Steadying my voice, I said, "Dad, did you ever see . . . anything?"

"Not me." He stood up, working the kinks out of his back. "You know how these old stories grow in the telling." But then he added, "I don't know what my mother thought. I know she didn't like to hear talk about that particular ghost. Too close to home, I suppose."

Then we were all too sleepy to make it through another moment. We pulled up the roof of the Ford and rolled the boys in car rugs to settle them on the backseat. They were joyous at turning in for the first time in their lives with dirty faces and necks. Dad drifted off, sitting bolt upright behind the wheel with his necktie in place. The rusty sound of the distant windpump turned in my dreams until daylight.

We made it to Grand Tower by the next afternoon, though we'd overheated at Rockwood. The road nearly played out past Fountain Bluff. Then we were coming down a last hill, above the town, steeping like tea in the deep summer damp.

Above the town Dad pointed out a long, sharp-backed hill as the Devil's Backbone. Across the river on the Missouri side another stone outcropping rose straight out of the water. This was Tower Rock, and it gave the town its name, Dad said.

The whole heat-hazed place looked as old as the rocks it nestled among. It didn't seem likely to me that anybody had ever been young here.

We drove up the Backbone as near to the house as we could get. I remember it now like a moving-picture show of that time, without sound and all in black and white.

I see the little old lady on the porch with her hands in her apron. Grandma Tilly: a tiny face wrinkled like a walnut, and wisps of hair drawn back in a knot. Behind her apron she's slender as a girl, and there's something young about her. She dances with the pleasure of seeing Dad stride up the hill. To her, he's "young Bill," we're young Bill's boys. She's been waiting for this moment.

Behind her in a rocker is her husband, older than she is, ancient. Waxy with age, trapped by the years and his chair, but alive behind his eyes. He has a shock of fine white hair and a curling, somehow military mustache. He wears a once-ivory alpaca suit in this stifling afternoon, and a high collar under his chins. He's too old to stand, but his loose-boned, veiny hand comes out to Dad, and his eyes are wet.

The camera of my memory ducks under the tin-roofed porch and enters the house as everybody did, through the kitchen door. A black iron range stands before the old open hearth. A door to the hall shows the way upstairs. There are big square bedrooms above, smelling of old times, and the old. A big chest of drawers stands in the upstairs hall. Beyond it in the best room that looks out on the river is Dad's aunt Delphine, in a four-poster bed.

The room hangs in lavender scent. It's so crowded with things, you could miss a smaller woman in the bed. But my great-aunt is very stout. Her hands, restless on the turned-back sheet, look like little pillows. Rings are embedded in her fingers. She's propped below a picture on the wall of a man with yellow hair in an old-fashioned costume.

She turns startling violet eyes on us. Under her beribboned bed cap, her black hair is in ringlets like a girl's. She has a faint mustache. When she sees my dad, her plump hands fly to her mouth, and the tears flow in dark streaks down her face.

In the moving picture memory makes, Great-uncle Noah is under the window of his wife's room, weeding one-handed in the heat of the day. But that can't be. The garden ran down from the far side of the house, and Uncle Noah would have been on the porch with his sister Tilly to greet us. He was certainly there on the day we left—only a little bent over, in his shirtsleeves, one of them pinned up above the missing arm.

In the first moments of our visit, even the little boys were all eyes. They'd been promised snakes around the woodshed and catfish they could catch themselves. They'd banked on shoeless days and bathless nights. But just for a moment they were caught in the grip of this place. They felt the weight of its history, and mystery.

So did I. The paper was loose and peeling on the walls. I wondered how many layers you'd have to scrape away until you came to the time when these old people were young. If they ever were.

I wondered how quiet you'd have to be to hear the voices of those times.

The House Astride the Devil's Backbone

1861

Chapter Two

"Tilly!" Mama called out to me from the kitchen. "Go find Cass."

The sun was winking away behind the big rock across the river. Tower Rock, standing high out of the water. A grove of trees grew over the top of it. Tower Rock rose on the other bank of the river and our Devil's Backbone here on the Illinois side. A dangerous stretch of river ran between—our stretch of the river.

Even though Tower Rock was over in Missouri, with the river between us, it gave our town its name: Grand Tower. Nobody wanted to live in a town named after the devil.

It wasn't any use to holler for Cass from the porch. Up in

her private places on her hill, she was deaf unto the world. Cass was a terrible worry to Mama, and I thought anything that worried Mama ought to worry me.

As quick as the sun was down, a chill came off the water. It was the end of April with some spring showing, time for the river to stir itself. Word had reached us that the ice was breaking up below St. Paul and rotting above Dubuque. We'd had the packet boats down from Quincy and St. Louis. But we needed the Southern boats to keep us in business. And only days ago President Abe Lincoln had proclaimed a blockade on the Southern ports.

Last month when Lincoln was inaugurated as the President of the United States, we'd built bonfires down by the landing to celebrate—show him the way to Washington, as people said. Few were for him, of course. You had to set fire to the woods and sift the ashes to find a Republican around here. But Lincoln was an Illinois man, one of us.

Now we didn't know what to think. The South was breaking away, and what did this blockade mean? If it meant shutting down the river traffic, it was serious. We heard Arkansas was ready to pull out of the Union, and St. Louis was in an uproar. So we saw trouble coming our way.

Cass had blazed the only paths there were to the crest of the hill. I made right for her. I always knew where to look for Cass. I just never knew what I'd find when I got there.

She was slumped on a flat rock we always called the devil's footstool, just among ourselves. From here you looked down through the trees to the landing and across the river too. You could see forever from here, though what Cass saw didn't bear thinking about.

She huddled in Mama's old threadbare shawl. Her face was wet with tears, gray as the sundown river. She was only twelve and looked ten. She'd just about give up on school, the winter took so much out of her. And thin? Not much more than breath and britches. The wind went straight through her, though we were both still sewed into our winter underwear.

That's the way we done in them days. You was sewed into your underwear in October and didn't see yourself again till late spring. We thought if we got nekkid and washed ourselves in the wintertime, we'd catch a chill that would carry us off.

"Oh, Cassy, for pity's sake," I said, big-sistering her. I flung down on the devil's footstool, and she let me hug her close. She looked up like she'd never laid eyes on me. Her eyes were too big for her face.

"Cassy, what now?"

"Dretful." She tucked her face into my shoulder. "All the dead and the dying. You can smell their wounds from here."

"Who this time?" I asked, but I didn't want to know. "Is it the wedding party?"

I hoped not. The wedding party was Grand Tower's oldest story. It went back to 1839, and people talked about it yet. It seemed there was a young couple who took a notion to get married across the river on top of Tower Rock. She was Miss Penelope Pike. He was John Randolph Davis, both of them shirttail kin to half the county. They set forth in an open boat with the bride's parents and sister, the groom's mother, and three slaves. The Reverend Josiah Maxwell went too, to tie the knot for them.

Well, they got married on the rock. Don't ask how they got up to the top of the thing. That's never part of the story. On their way back, their boat was caught crossways in the current and pulled down by a whirlpool. They disappeared without a trace, though a moment before they were visible from both shores. That was the story of the wedding party. The problem was that Cass often saw them.

From up here where she nested, she'd catch sight of them, pushing off in an old-timey boat. There'd be the bride, wearing her veil crowned with orange blossom. There'd be the groom behind her, splitting the seams on his best coat to help with the rowing. There they'd be in the bright morning of all their hopes. To hear her tell it, Cass saw them as clear as if she'd been one of the party.

It could get a lot worse than that. Cass had seen the wedding party return. She saw them after the whirlpool had drawn them down to the bottom of the river. Now they were pulling hard for this shore in their swamped boat, pulling and pulling and never making it. She saw them caked in silt, their hands tangled with weed. She saw their gray corpse faces eaten away by the fish. The bridal veil snagged in the bride's skeleton shoulder. She saw their ghosts.

"No, Tilly." Cass pulled back from me. "Not this time,

though it was in April when they was drowned." Her face was solemn and smudgy. Evening was drawing in on us, even here at the top of the Backbone.

"Was it the old Spaniards?" I said. "Or the Frenchies?" Many a time she'd seen them too. She said she had.

She'd seen the first explorers on this river, though they'd come two hundred years ago, maybe more. She could tell you everything about them, describe to you every chink in their queer foreign boats. She could smell the hogs the Spaniards brought to feed themselves.

She saw the Frenchmen coming down from the northern lakes in their pirogues. They were dressed in Chinese costume, for they were looking for China and expected it around every bend in the river. She could call these ancients by name, though she hadn't learned them at school. She paid very little attention at school.

These old explorers were never just drifting peacefully past, not in Cass's visions. She saw them caught in the quick drain of a whirlpool. She saw their sudden, swirling deaths far from home, all hands lost before they could know. She heard the hogs squealing their last.

Sometimes it was the Indians who died. Though they were wiser to the river than foreigners, the eddies between our rocks could claim them too. Their swift, slender canoes folded like paper. Hands upflung, they were swept in a circle out of sight. They were the Miamis, Cass said, though how could she know?

She sobbed in my arms till my shoulder was wet. She was

worse this time. Was she getting worse? I looked away, down to the landing. It reached out in the water, lanterns lit to lead the boats that hadn't come.

Mama feared that people were commencing to talk about Cass. She never told her visions outside the family. She said little or nothing in company. But people could see her up here, perched on the Devil's Backbone. Before the trees greened, they could see her plain, staring out at the river like a soul in torment. They called her moony. Mama feared they'd one day call her mad.

Then what could be done about her?

I'd have to get her home now, though she was blind with tears. "Cass, tell me who you see now. Who do you mourn? Who were the dead and the dying this time?"

She liked to work free of me, pulling away from her own visions. You could tell they were a knife to her heart. "All the boys," she keened. "Just boys, blown apart, blue and gray."

When she said they were blue and gray, I thought she meant their cold, drowned faces. Maybe I thought that.

"Too young," she moaned. "Boats burdened with them, and blood in the water behind."

She'd seen steamboats blow up too, many a time. But who hadn't? The big steamboats blew up often enough, six or eight right near us that I could remember: the *Ida May* and the *Little Jim Reese* and the *Belle of St. Louis* among them. The boilers would cut loose and rip the rickety contraptions to splinters and smithereens. Bodies boiled alive would wash ashore for days after. But we'd all seen that.

"When did it happen, Cass?"

She looked at me with eyes more haunted than her heart. "It ain't happened yet," she said.

I went cold to my core. All her visions looked back, sometimes to ages past. Now she'd whipped around and was looking ahead. And that was the April when we all feared the future. It was the spring of 1861, when all the news was bad, promising worse.

She was limp as a rag. I gathered her up and dabbed at her eyes with the shawl. As we drew nigh the house, Noah, our brother, was climbing the hill, home for his supper.

Noah had grown tall as a stork, seemingly overnight. His knees were working through his britches, and his wrists grown out of his sleeves. He stalked up through the trees with Paw's old fowling piece on his shoulder. The gun was older than the shoulder that bore it. The barrel was scabby with rust. But Noah had been marching and drilling with it.

A bunch of local boys met up after their work, pretending to soldier. You couldn't get many boys to stick up for U. S. Grant and the North that April. Only the Henson boys and Gideon Hickman and Jack Popejoy. And Noah.

You could hear them from up here, barking out their raggedy commands: "Draw saber! By the right flank, quick trot, march!" Like they knew all about it. They marched with whatever they had—a squirrel rifle, a corn knife, a paling off the porch. They looped lariats at their sides, for leading home a reb prisoner-of-war.

Down the road by the old stone structure that served as

schoolhouse, a bigger bunch of boys drilled. But they drilled for the South and Jeff Davis. Among them, the Cottrell brothers and Mose Thornton and Jaret Dalrymple. And Curry Marshall.

They'd divvied up, some for the North, more for the South. Why didn't they just fight it out right here in the road, fair and square? Did they even know it could end with them killing one another in some godforsaken loblolly far from home? I couldn't get my mind around it, and I'd always thought I understood Noah. We were twins, and I swore I could hear his heart beat.

Coming along behind me, Cass caught sight of him. She let out a startled cry, and I thought she'd bolt. Instead, she burst into fresh tears and heaved with sobs. Both hands covered her face. I had to lead her home.

Chapter Three

By the time Noah come in from the pump, we pretty nearly had supper on the table. Cass was good help if you could keep her mind on it. She could cook water-ground meal and make clabber milk and bone a mudfish as well as Mama herself. She knew her herbs too, what they seasoned and what they cured. She knew her black root and golden-seal and lady slipper and prickly ash, and where to find them.

Cass took charge of the chickens too. They lived penned up on the other side of the house. Chickens and me didn't get along. If I had to keep them, I'd as soon not eat them.

But Cass had a hand with fowl. She named them too, every chick of them, before they feathered out. Mama said better not name anything you're fixing to eat. But Cass did. She went right on naming them, under her breath.

We thought we et pretty good. Noah was right smart to kill game: squirrel and prairie chickens and in the fall before it wintered up, possum. Quail, pheasant, ducks. We baked corn dodgers and fried meat in the fireplace. But white beans, gristle, and cornmeal mush got us through the darkest part of winter. Here in April we were still weeks from anything out of our garden.

Oh, you can't picture how we lived back then. There wasn't but a string latch on the door. And we didn't have a stove of any description. I'd never seen one. We kindled fires with flint and steel and cooked over an open flame in the kitchen. We baked in a Dutch oven set into the bricks beside the hearth. In the winter we lived in this kitchen to keep warm. That's how it was with us. We didn't know any better.

Noah hung Paw's fowling piece with the pouch and the shotbag on the chimney. Mama wanted him to sit at the head of the table, in Paw's chair. It was to remind Noah that he was all the man this family had.

We turned back our sleeves and fell to our supper. Mama had seen Cass's red, swollen, staring eyes. Noah was his silent self. Most times, he could make a tree seem talkative. I heard a distant rumble over the river and hoped it was thunder.

Long before people began hollering war, Mama was already afraid she'd lose Noah. Most boys hankered to go on the river. They'd hang around the landing, wanting to be taken on as roustabouts. They dreamed their boy-dreams of being steersmen, which was what apprentice pilots were called. They'd have settled for being strikers, wiping down the metalwork with oily rags. The names of the boats swam in their heads: the *Gray Eagle,* the *Jubilee,* the *Neptune,* the *Rowena,* the *Fashion,* the *Vesuvius,* the *Arkansas Star.* What a worry this had always been to Mama.

A darker cloud gathered over her last Christmastime when South Carolina seceded from the Union. They'd get the *Cairo City Gazette* down at the landing, only a day or so late. We weren't backwoodsy people who still didn't know Lincoln was President. The minute Mama heard that the cotton states were seceding, she feared anew for Noah.

Then this month when Little Napoleon Beauregard fired on Fort Sumter in Charleston Bay, the whole sky darkened. Another week and Lincoln had proclaimed his blockade of the Southern ports. Now he was calling for seventy-five thousand volunteers to fight.

Mama couldn't spare Noah. But she couldn't forbid him much longer. Him and me would be sixteen in the fall. He was a good boy, steadier than Paw. But he was restless as a riderless horse.

We et our meal by the light of the kitchen fire. Mama looked up once, stole a glance at Noah. But he was only a dark, broad-shouldered shape against the crackling fire.

It was big doings that night, a dance in the room over Rodgers's store. This was the first such gathering of the spring. A fiddler was in from Cobden, and Mr. Chilly Atabury to do the calling.

We wore our other dresses, the linsey ones we tried to save back. Noah wore an old black coat of Paw's, and he was lost in it. We went, though. Everybody in the district who wasn't tied to the bed or locked in the attic went. Everybody would be there, bar the riffraff who lived around the ruins of a still, south of town.

Mama thought we ought to make a showing. She didn't want people talking behind our backs. She didn't want talk against Paw, or Cass. Mama had her pride, though she said herself that pride could hollow you out.

Grand Tower was only a settlement in them days, somewhere between a landing and a town. They hadn't gotten around to a survey of the place. It was mainly strung along a single dirt road we called Front Street. People said that if war come to us, it would either make Grand Tower or break it.

Many an old plug workhorse stood at the rail outside Rodgers's store. Fiddle music whined from the upper windows. Upstairs, we found the room crowded under the yellow tallow light.

Mama made for the mourners' bench where the older women sat out, looking on. There were sets already dancing down the room and another square going at the end with the young kids. But Cass stuck close to Mama. Cass wouldn't mix, and there wasn't anything you could do about it.

Mama was still young enough to shake a leg. But Paw wasn't there. Old Aunt Madge Bledsoe made room between herself and an aged country woman named Mrs. Harod Yancey. It was her whose sister-in-law, Mrs. Champ Hazelrigg, was et by her own hogs. Mrs. Yancey was old-fashioned even for them days and dipped snuff on a stick to rub on her gums. With a quick nod Mama settled in with Cass beside her.

Noah and me hung at the edges, watching the dancing. There was no shame in partnering with your brother, but it took Noah time to set his mind to it.

Mr. Chilly Attabury was in full spate, calling,

Bird in,
Buzzard in,
Pretty good bird
For the shape she's in.

Hands clapped, elbows flapped, and that old sprung floor rolled and heaved. Mr. Chilly Attabury could grow topical in his calling:

Buchanan out,
Give a shout!
Lincoln in,
Show a shin!

People whooped at that, and fashioned footwork to go with it. But then he went too far as he was apt to do when he called,

Jeff Davis is a President,
Abe Lincoln is a fool,
Jeff Davis rides a big bay horse,
Abe Lincoln rides a mule.

Jeff Davis had just been made President of this new country the Southerners—the Secesh—thought they'd started up, and Lincoln was our own Illinois man. The Southerners whooped with approval. Catcalls and heavy stomping came from the rest.

Mr. Attabury drew up just shy of a fistfight and fell back on an old faithful, "Texas Star":

Gents to the center
And back to the bar,
Ladies to the center
To form the star.

Now we were in there with them, me and Noah, backing and forthing and sashaying with the rest. I tried to switch my meager skirts and find my place as the star turned to the tune.

Then somehow I was across from that young man named Curry Marshall. Now our elbows linked, so I tried to grow light on my feet. I bit my lips to make them pink, and tried to simper. But I expect Curry Marshall was looking straight over my head. He was a big, tall galoot, tall as Noah.

I don't know how long we all danced until, like the crack of doom, a steamboat whistle split the air. The bow bounced off the fiddle, and everybody stomped to a sudden stop.

Right quick we heard footsteps pounding up the stairs. T. W. Jenkins burst upon us. "It's a Southern boat! It's the *Rob Roy* from out of New Orleans!"

A whoop went up from the Southerners and Northerners alike. "Where's my boys?" cried T. W. Jenkins. He ran the freight landing and the store that went with it, the only other store we had.

There was unloading to be done, of whatever was coming off the boat. Noah and Curry Marshall and three or four others who worked at the freight landing darted forward. Noah brought home the only ready money we had, though Mama thought he worked too close to the river.

Everybody ganged down the stairs. We met every boat, and this was a special case. The clammy night air hit us full in the face as all the town made for the landing. The *Rob Roy* blazed with lamplight that lit the water around it. The paddle wheel churned in reverse. The gangplank was already down. I'd never set foot on a big boat. To me a riverboat was a palace. The pair of flaring gold chimney stacks belched flame-colored smoke into the night. Below them the decks glowed like a gingerbread wedding cake.

The *Rob Roy* was full to the gills with passengers. They must have been Yankees hurrying home in case war trapped them. And there were those people who seemed always on the river, restless travelers. The railings were jammed tight with dark figures. I saw the firefly glow of the gentlemen's seegars. I imagined I saw diamonds within the ladies' flowing cloaks, and emeralds in their hair.

I couldn't picture where they'd come from, where they were going. Did I know enough to wonder?

We worked our way forward to see Noah and Curry and the other boys running up the gangplank for the freight. We all waved and waved till the pilot up on the Texas deck bother to wave back. What a sight it all was, this brilliance in the velvet night.

People were crazy to hear the news. They called up to the passengers leaning on the rails. "What's it like down yonder? What's conditions at New Orleans?"

"Port's open!" someone called back. "Business as usual. Still shippin' cotton. But we was boarded and searched at Cairo."

We drank it all in and turned over every word. Then lo and behold, two figures were coming down the plank. Will I ever forget that first sight of them? Two figures, backlit by the boat, come down to us by lantern light.

A young lady was in the lead, in ballooning crinolines. Heavens, I'd never seen such skirts—rustling taffeta stretched wide over hoops. Her top part was encased in a cut-plush cape, with tassels. And her bonnet. My stars, I pushed people aside to get a look at it. A bonnet too dark to make out except for the ice-blue satin it was lined with, and a whole corsage of artificial violets planted inside next to her face. An enormous satin bow tied beneath her chin.

And then her face, framed with long dark curls beside the violets. Her eyes were large and darkly fringed. Her Cupid's bow of a mouth too dark to be as nature intended. She must be from New Orleans. No town between here and there could have produced her.

The slant of the gangplank all but upturned her. She clung to the rope with one gloved hand. From the other hung a round hatbox covered in elegant wallpaper.

She turned back to the young woman behind her. I saw this other one only in silhouette at first. She was narrower, darker, shrouded in a long plain cloak. In place of a bonnet or a traveling hat, her head was tied up in a bandanna. It was of some fine silken material, and the tails of the knot were artfully arranged. Her hands were full of various boxes and reticules. The two of them murmured together.

Behind them a deckhand staggered under a humpbacked Saratoga trunk. At the end of the plank he very nearly stepped through the young lady's hoops. When he swung the trunk off his back, it lit in the mud.

By then, I was standing as close to the young lady as I am to you. She turned right to me. *"Il est saoul!"* she said. Her great fringed eyes grew wider.

"Come again?" I said, in a trance.

"He's drunk, that one. All men are drunkards! And the

men on this boat, all of them spit, spit, spit." She pointed back to the *Rob Roy* in case I'd missed seeing it.

I stared at her, and all the crowd around us stood silent, listening in.

Drunk or sober, the deckhand was back up the plank. Now here he came again with yet another trunk. I'd never known anybody with two trunkloads of anything.

But no, wait. It was Noah, bent under this second trunk. He sidestepped the young lady and almost fell off the plank for looking at her.

She noticed him, I believe. But now she turned to address us all. Evidently, the world was her stage. "I am meant for St. Louis, but I cannot go on! It is too dangerous there," she sang out, and in her mouth, the word *dangerous* took on quite a foreign sound.

It was true there was unrest up there. On the day Lincoln took his oath of office, a Confederate flag was rung up over the Berthold mansion in St. Louis. Confederate flags rose above some of the best houses on Olive Street, according to word we'd had. People said the only safeguard to Federal authority in Missouri was the St. Louis arsenal. Soon, people said, there'd be blood in the streets.

"I am, how do you say it?" the young lady declared. "Out of the frying pan and into the fire!"

What must we all have looked like to her, listening open-mouthed to her every word? It didn't seem to displease her. "And I was insulted at Cairo!" She looked around at us with her great fringed eyes to see how we took this terrible news.

Cairo was the last town at the bottom tip of Illinois, where the North points a long finger at the South.

"Insulted," she repeated. "Me!" She dealt her bosom a blow. "The Federals, they come on the boat in a swarm like bees. They want to see our papers. They want to count our money. They go through our things." She pointed out her trunks and shook her hatbox at us. "I was so scare I poosh a scream!"

Darker than the night, her eyes widened to fill her bonnet. "They look at things no man should see!"

We stirred.

"And would you believe! They take from me my pistol!" We caught our breaths. She'd been armed?

"Hardly more than a toy! A lady's pistol that live in my muff! I am desolated without it. How handy a pistol can be, and mine had a pearl handle!"

Now we were struck dumber than before.

"No, we cannot brave St. Louis." She swept a tiny gloved hand back at the other young woman, the silent one. "I was meant to pay a visit to my aunt, Madame LeBlanc." Again the young lady's gaze swept us. "Madame Blanche LeBlanc. She is known to you?"

We only gaped silently back, our tongues tied.

Was this young lady an actress? I for one wondered. I'd heard about the playacting on the showboats. But surely no performance to beat this one.

"We cannot go on. It is as if we are . . . *naufrage* . . . how do you say it? Shipwrecked! We stay here. Is there a hotel?"

Transfixed though we were, we'd been watching the young woman behind her too. The darker one. She must be a servant. Was she a slave? A question murmured among us. Was she a slave standing now on the free soil of Illinois? My, how we wondered.

"You won't care much for the hotel," old Aunt Madge Bledsoe called out. Leave it to Aunt Madge. And she wasn't wrong. We had what we called a hotel for the salesmen and agents coming off the boats. It was even grandly named "the St. James." But it was only four rooms over a saloon that sold 'shine and red-eye. And it was said that the bedroom walls didn't reach all the way to the ceiling.

"No, it wouldn't do for you," someone else said. I looked around, and it was Mama, with Cass in hand. You could have knocked me over with a feather. Mama rarely spoke out. "You-uns can come stay with me. It's plain, but they's room."

The young lady considered. "I can pay," she said.

Mama nodded while our world listened.

"Me, I am Delphine Duval," the young lady said to Mama. "And here is Calinda." She gestured at the figure behind her, in her shadow.

"I'm Mrs. Pruitt," Mama said.

"Enchantée, madame," said Delphine Duval. She put out her small hand, and Mama took it.

"I'm Tilly Pruitt," I said, speaking right up. "This here's my sister, Cass." I had to speak for Cass. She wouldn't say boo to a goose, unless it had come back from the dead.

Delphine Duval dropped a small curtsy my way, and I felt her eyes take me on. I looked past her to the other girl, to Calinda. "Tilly Pruitt," I said to her, putting out my hand. But hers were full, and she didn't nod. I couldn't see her shadowed eyes.

Noah was there by now, very red in the face, no doubt from hauling the freight.

"That there is my twin brother, Noah," I explained, because in the presence of Delphine Duval he was all eyes and no tongue. But he hefted her trunk back onto his shoulder. Cass and I managed the other trunk between us. As the boat began to move away, churning water behind us, the crowd parted, and off we went. Calinda was hung all over with parcels and valises. Delphine was only lightly burdened by her hatbox.

Mama led the way because it was dark as a snake's insides now. I watched the shape of Delphine's swaying, sighing hoopskirts and saw that her slippers had heels, as we climbed the Devil's Backbone, heading for home.

I couldn't see a moment ahead.

Chapter Four

Oh, that Delphine give me a hard night! I tossed and turned, still seeing her come down the plank in all her New Orleans finery, like a visitor from the moon.

It wasn't every day in the week that we had company in our spare room. They'd seemed to expect a candle, so we give them one. I thrashed in the bed, wondering if they'd burn down the house. I was so restless that even Cass, who slept in the trundle at the foot of my bed, reared up to see what ailed me. And Cass could sleep through earthquake, famine, and flood—another of her peculiarities.

Just before dawn, Mama nearly scared me into a fit by coming in the room and looming over my bed. Her hair let down swept my face, just as I'd been dreaming of lace and gauzy silk.

"Listen to me," Mama whispered. "I don't dare to talk out loud." She jerked her head to the wall between our room and the room where Delphine and Calinda were. "I don't know what to make of them two," said Mama. "Be real careful what you say around them. Watch every word. I think that Calinda might be a slave, and I wonder if that Delphine knows which side of the river they's on. Don't explain a thing, even if asked."

She gave the corner of my quilt a twitch to make sure I attended every whispered word. I nodded in the night. A law on the books said that black people weren't allowed into Illinois. We paid no attention to that, of course. There were plenty of black people in the state. And they were all free.

Mama melted away. As quick as she was out in the hall, she let forth a shriek to wake the dead. Through the crack in the door, I saw she'd walked straight into Calinda. In the gloom, the tails of her bandanna stood up like perky ears. She was dressed for the day, evidently.

Then I heard Mama say, "Oh, well, yes. They's plenty of hot water for washing yourselves." The two of them went off downstairs to the kitchen fire. Once more, Cass reared up in the trundle and blinked around in the dark. I may have dozed because the next thing I remember is daylight in the kitchen.

Mama and I bustled. Today we had guests, and paying

ones at that. Besides, Mama liked things done right, poor though we were. She'd come from up around Vandalia when it was the capital of the state. She knew how things ought to be, so we got out a cloth for the table, a blue-and-white checked, much darned and patched.

I laid the table. Mama was frying scrapple and two eggs apiece for us all, like Christmas morning. We couldn't afford coffee, but she brewed up a big pot of our sassafras tea. We dug the sassafras root out in the timber, and dried the bark.

Mama had sent Cass upstairs to say that breakfast was about on the table. Cass was no sooner there than she was back again. She shot into the kitchen like a pack of hounds was on her tail. Her mouth was stretched in a wordless scream, and she was as gray-faced as the ghosts she often saw. She grabbed the edge of the table, then fetched up a breath and howled out, "The tall one's killin' the short one!"

Mama dropped the spatula and spun around, supposing that Cass had finally lost all her reason. "I'm tellin' you!" Cass yelled. "Calinda's killin' the little fancy one, and the little one's hurtin' bad!"

Hearing Cass at the top of her lungs brought Noah out from the room he slept in down here behind the chimney. He was shaking off sleep and wondering who was being killed.

"Cass, is this one of your visions," I said, "or is it real?"

She stamped a foot. "It's happenin', dadburn it!"

Mama gave Cass a searching look. Then we all bolted out of the kitchen, along the hall, up the stairs. Cass was in the lead, and Noah brought up the rear. Mama stopped halfway up and turned on him. "Not you, boy. You go back. There might be nekkidness this early in the day."

The door to the spare room stood ajar. Of our three bedrooms upstairs, this was the best, looking out across to Tower Rock. We heard sighs and whimpers. Delphine was evidently still alive, if barely.

Mama went forth, and we let her. She stalked into the spare room and pulled up short. "Oh for the land's sake!" she said, whipping around to turn us back. I was naturally all eyes and saw everything.

Delphine stood, feet planted, at the foot of the big old four-poster bed. Both her hands grabbed the poster tight. Mama had been right to forbid Noah this sight. Delphine wore not a stitch but white cotton stockings, her drawers, and corsets.

Behind her was Calinda with one foot on the floor and the other foot in the small of Delphine's back. With both hands Calinda was pulling tight the straining strings of the corsets, like the reins on a rearing horse. Straining and straining and just about cutting poor, gasping Delphine in two to draw her corsets tight enough so you could span her waist with two hands.

Now we were out in the hall, making tracks. As a rule, Mama went easy on Cass. But today, she gave her ear a good wrenching. "Girl, I'd like to turn you every way but loose," she said. "She wasn't killing her. She was getting her into her corsets."

"Well, I never seen nothing like it," Cass whined.

Neither had I, and I'd sooner be murdered than to have to wear a pair of them corset things. "Mama," I said, "did you ever wear them?"

"Once on the day I was married, and that was plenty. I passed out twice before I got to the altar."

We were on the stairs now. Mercifully neither Calinda nor Delphine had made note of us in their room. We hadn't lingered. Still, I was amazed at their clutter. Both trunks yawned, and the room was festooned with all manner of clothes and I don't know what all.

"They must have been calculating a long visit to St. Louis," I said.

"If you ask me," Mama murmured, "them two don't add up."

Noah stood by the kitchen fire with a mug of tea in his hand, as wide-eyed with wonder as he ever got.

"No harm done," said Mama, "and nothing to concern you." Pointing him into Paw's chair, she straightened her apron and went back to the skillet.

We sat to our breakfast, not knowing how long the corset business would last. While short, Delphine was not small.

"Heavens above," I muttered, "does she go through that torture every morning of her life?" But Mama narrowed her eyes at me because Noah was sopping up every word.

We'd set two places for our company. I don't know if you could call Mama abolitionist or not. But she took a very dim view of slavery and slave owners, and didn't care who knew it. In the state of Illinois, even this far south, Calinda would sit at the table like the rest of us. I wondered where she'd slept. There was but one big bed in the room. Did slaves sleep on the floor? Seemed like there wasn't room for a cat to nap with all their tangle strewn about.

Then there they were at the door. Delphine was first. After my last glimpse of her, I couldn't believe this one. That was no more her natural waist than it was mine. But, goodness, how tiny and dainty it was. Skirts flared below it, so wide she could hardly pass through the door.

Above, she was hung with several fine shawls. She peered curiously into the room. We peered curiously back. Her skin was perfect, and there was powder on her face. You could see it. But she hadn't chanced paint here in the cold light of dawn. Her lips were pale. There were patches of a naturally violet color below her dark eyes. We saw her full-face now, without her bonnet.

How had Calinda managed her young lady's hair? The black curls hung long to frame her face.

"Bonjour, mes amis," she remarked, and floated forth. Calinda followed. A white bandanna would have made her face darker. This one was of a color we used to call guinea blue. White scarves crossed the top of her dress. She was as narrow-faced as Delphine was round. But they had the same eyes, though Calinda's trusted no one.

Mama looked at Noah, and he was suddenly on his feet. The chair fell over behind him. Cass and I were at the fire, bringing breakfast. Calinda settled beside Mama as if she expected to be there. That put Delphine next to Noah. He hadn't stood behind their chairs to seat them, as Mama pointed out to him later. Now he'd retrieved his chair. It was as well he was sitting again because he was weak in the knees.

We slid the plates before them. Mama had made a name for herself with her scrapple. It was cornmeal and shredded pork off the neck bones. You gelled this mess in a long pan and kept it in a cool place. Then you sliced out slabs of it to fry in lard. Today Mama had used butter instead. I could eat my weight in scrapple. The eggs were done to a turn.

I leaned in to pour brimming cups of sassafras tea. Calinda bent to sniff at her cup, and flinched. Overlooking her eggs, Delphine said, "How good you are to take us in, orphans of the storm." Her smile was like sunup. Across from me, Calinda eyed the scrapple with dark suspicion. She poked at an egg with her fork.

"I hope you slept," Mama remarked. Her face was damp from the fire. Seeing Delphine's hair, she just touched her own.

"Mais oui, madame," Delphine said. "We stuff petticoats around the windows. We wear our cloaks."

Cass went goggle-eyed and surprised herself into speech: " 'Tain't winter!"

No, it was springtime. We slept with the windows wide open. On the other hand, we were still sewn into our winter underwear. And as we knew, Delphine, for one, wasn't.

Her laugh tinkled like silver. "Yet it is more winter than we know." I saw they were both still freezing. Tomorrow, I thought, I'll put them nearer the fire, to thaw them.

That was the way with Delphine. You tried to think of ways to please her. I saw that on the first day.

We weren't used to talk at the table, and the kitchen rang with hers. She babbled and bubbled like a wellspring, and told nothing. Her accent came and went. I looked back to the way life had been yesterday, and couldn't find it.

Dazzled though I was, I saw Calinda wasn't going near her breakfast. Delphine moved more vittles around her plate than she ate. The sparkle of her gaze played back and forth over us, always ending to linger on Noah. She saw how red his ears had gone. Who could miss them? They were on fire.

He didn't chance a look at her, but he drank in every word. If she'd reached out and touched his wrist, he might have fallen forward in a faint. A scent came from her, of some flower we didn't know. Noah swayed.

Mama saw and didn't like it. All men were what she called "susceptible," and Noah thought he was a man already. Mama stepped in, so to speak. "Won't your aunt up at St. Louis wonder what become of you?"

Calinda shot a quick sideways glance at Delphine, who answered at once. "*Tante Blanche!* Of course, unless she is already murder in her bed. I write at once to say where we are." Now she did touch Noah's wrist. "Where are we? Me, I know nothing. What is this place?"

Noah swallowed. "All the territory this end of the state's called Egypt, and this here is Grand Tower."

"It thrives, this place?"

Noah rubbed his chin to make the point that he shaved. "It's promising." He pitched his voice way down below his bootlaces. "If we could get the railroad in here, we could load the boats with the coal coming out of Mount Carbon and Murphysboro. A rail line could make us, might could bring in some industry. The railroad first reached the river up at Rock Island and made a considerable town of it."

I fell back in the chair. That was the longest speech that ever come out of that boy's mouth. Was he running for office? But then Cass was chirpier too this morning. We were all changed, overnight.

Mama didn't draw breath until Delphine's hand slipped back in her lap. Noah went on looking at his wrist where her fingers had been.

"And your folks down South," Mama pressed on, "won't they fret over your whereabouts?"

Delphine started in her chair, prettily. "*Maman!* But naturally I must write her. Will the next boat take the letter? She will be beside herself until she know we are safe."

"I wonder your mother didn't come with you since things are so . . . unsettled down there." Mama was beginning to pry for sure.

"Ah, she is brave, that one," Delphine said. "If anyone dare besiege New Orleans, Clemence Duval will defend it with her last breath. Who will not? Let the enemy smell the gunpowder of Louis Hébert's Pelican rifles. All that gold braid! You know what happen in that War of 1812 when *les maudits Anglais* try to take New Orleans? They—how you say it? Skedaddle."

She glanced at Paw's fowling piece hanging there above Noah's head. I had a quick picture of her mother up there on a levee with her skirts in her boots and a rifle butt in her shoulder, taking potshots at us Yankees.

Delphine turned over a tiny, plump hand. "But war may not come to us. New Orleans is the largest city of the South, perhaps the greatest in the world. It could strangle the North by blocking to ships the river's mouth." She knotted her fist and held it up. "New York will do anything to keep our cotton coming. New York does not care who picks it."

She leaned nearer, to take us into her confidence. "*Maman* is a lady of fashion, you know. To our house on Chartres Street come all the persons of tone, all the distinguished." She sketched that house in the air for us to see, and I swear I did. "*Maman's* loge is on the second tier of the French Opera House, the grand new one on Bourbon Street. When she is driven out the Chalmette Road to take the air, crowds form."

Delphine caught her breath at her mother's magnificence. "Tall as a swaying palmetto is *Maman,* the belle of ev'ry ball. You have not live until you see *Maman* revolving in the waltz, her shoulders bare, her throat ablaze. They cannot hold the opera on Wednesday nights. Clemence

Duval is at the ball! The balls, you know, each Wednesday at the Salle d'Orleans."

Something happened then. Below the table Calinda's hand seemed to jerk at Delphine's skirts. Delphine fell silent. A warning had passed between them. We all noticed. Well, maybe not Noah.

Delphine wavered and went on. "No, *Maman* will not leave her *Nouvelle Orléans.* Not yet. Perhaps never. Perhaps we can all be as we were." She looked away from us, seeming to hear music.

That was Delphine all over. She could tell you so much that you thought you'd heard it all. Her conversation was a lacework fan that opened and closed, concealing and revealing. I didn't doubt her mother was rich and beautiful and admired. What other mother would Delphine have? What could be left to know?

We'd never lingered over breakfast this long in our lives. But Delphine stirred first. *"Eh bien,"* she said with a little shrug. "Well, me, I would like to examine the town. Are there shops?"

Chapter Five

It took the morning for Delphine and Calinda to unpack. Mama and Cass and I heard the thump and scrape of their trunks from above, and the mumble of their voices. Scents this house had never known drifted down to us: the sweetgrass of their baskets, the lavender of sachets. Who knew what came tumbling out of those treasure chests? I wouldn't have minded a look but it was none of my business.

So it was well past midday before Delphine and me started down the hill. Mama had turned me loose, and Calinda had said, "Me, I stay at 'ome"—the first time I ever heard her voice.

Best of all, I wore a bonnet of Delphine's—a store bonnet—when she saw I didn't own one. Hers was crowned with a spray of silk roses like the ones in the pattern of her dress. My bonnet was deep, so I saw the world at the end of a tunnel. I hoped to be noticed in it.

As quick as we were in Rodgers's store, we were watched like hawks—both Rodgerses and Pegleg Snelson and all their other help, and a couple of country women turning over the goods. Word of our visitors had reached well beyond Grand Tower by now.

Delphine made short work of the store. I feared that very little in it would interest her, and very little did. She breezed by the pile of mackinaw blankets. She barely browsed the dressmaking counter with its needles and pins, the ferreting for binding, the tin suspender buttons, and the dozen bolts of calico at seven cents a yard.

She turned up her pert nose at the maple sugar in lumps and swept past the home remedies, the liniments and laudanum and borax, and all the salves and sulfurs. We were shortly back out on the porch.

As Delphine could see, we'd pretty well done the town. Across the road was the only brick building, the office to lure Dr. Hutchings to come and doctor us. I for one wanted to give that place a wide berth. They said his floors were painted red to hide the blood.

Delphine nodded past this landmark to the freight landing. T. W. Jenkins ran a hardware and ship repair establishment beside it, along with a lumberyard and smithy.

"It is where your brother works, no?" Delphine said. "We go there."

I explained to her that womenfolk didn't go into Jenkins's as a rule. The forge was in a back room, and men were apt to hang around there, chewing and using language we all knew but weren't supposed to.

"Pffft," said Delphine, and lifted her skirts across the road.

On the porch of Jenkins's store, Mr. Clarence Worthen and Old Man "Dutchy" Brunckhorst were going at it, hammer and tongs. The Worthens' ancestry was Kentuckian, and they still called themselves Southern. Old Man Brunckhorst was straight from the old country and staunch for the Union and Lincoln. Each had a finger in the other's face.

We sidled past them and inside. It was far better stocked than Rodgers's. But here were cattle yokes and boat pins, oakum and caulking chisels and black iron pots. Hanging from rafters were rat traps and briar scythes and I don't know what all. I could see Noah in the yard behind, measuring off planking. I expected Delphine to turn on her heel. She rapped the counter for service.

As luck would have it, Curry Marshall answered the call. I looked away, to give him the side view of my bonnet. Then I looked square at him. Searching the contents of the bonnet, he found my face. "Hey, Tilly," he said.

I replied in kind. But I couldn't command much of his attention this near Delphine. She had a powerful effect on the male sex.

"Have you—how you say it? *Les allumettes?*" She spoke in a throaty voice. What she was doing with her eyes, I couldn't see.

Curry swallowed hard. "Zoom whats?" he said in a fading tone.

"To make fire." Delphine gestured.

"Matches," Curry said. "We do, but they's high."

Delphine overlooked that. "And lamps? Coal oil lamps?"

"They's higher than a cat's back. We want an arm and a leg for them." Curry hooked his thumbs into his shop apron.

Delphine overlooked that too. Evidently in New Orleans the merchants didn't warn you that their goods might be higher than you could pay.

"Send six or eight to the house of Madame Pruitt," Delphine said. "And the oil and the wicks and the chimneys. Plenty of oil, and a box of . . . matches."

Curry and I both gaped. I was all bonnet and jaw. Nobody but the doctor burned oil.

Curry recovered. "I'll box it up and bring it to the house, after work."

"Do not let darkness fall," warned Delphine.

There was some afternoon left. "Now we climb your hill," Delphine said, "to regard the view."

I told her it was liable to be muddy underfoot and spoil her petticoats. But that naturally didn't matter to her. We climbed the Backbone, past our house. Delphine showed a good deal of ankle, hitching her skirts over root and rock.

"How steep your country is." She began to puff. All her shawls were askew. When we came at last to the devil's footstool, I saw Cass wasn't there. As a rule, she'd escaped from the house by this time of day.

Delphine settled beside me on the footstool, and her skirts fell easy about her. How I admired her grace, and wondered how to have it.

The river flowed empty below, high with the spring floods from the snowmelt above us. Delphine nodded north. Between the Devil's Backbone and Oven Rock was a straggling graveyard.

"Your papa," she said. "He is there?"

"Oh no, Paw's not dead." Not that we knew of. She'd thought Mama was a widow woman.

"Paw's a river man. Summers, he works the logging camps up in the Minnesota country. Winters, he's down south, going shares on a seine net. A lot of the menfolk do that. They's here in the spring to put in the crops and back in the fall for the harvest. Of course, we haven't got any land, so they's no crops to put in."

Oh, I babbled like a brook and flowed like a freshet. At least I didn't tell her how many seasons had passed since we'd seen hide or hair of Paw. Years, really.

She seemed to hear more than I'd told. I was provoked at myself. Hadn't Mama just warned me to watch every word

I spoke? Hadn't she made that crystal clear? So I made so bold as to ask if Delphine had a paw.

"*Papa? Mais oui.* He is Monsieur Jules Duval. No doubt Mayor Duval by now, gird for war.

"I bring *Papa's* portrait in a gilt frame," she said. "I am never without it. You will see where it hangs over my bed."

He's apt to be hanging by the neck from a sour apple tree when us Yankees take New Orleans, I thought, but didn't say.

On Delphine flowed. "*Papa* is of an ancient French family, you know. The Duvals are there on their land long before the Americans come. Long before."

It took her no time to make me see the vast sweep of Duval cotton fields stretching for miles back from the river. She raised before my very eyes the columns that held up their deep porches, white as marble in the dazzling day. I saw the great houses of the Duvals standing in gardens hung with Spanish moss.

"He live, *Papa,* mostly in the country. A gentleman, you know. But he come to New Orleans for the opera, and of course for the balls.

"Ah, ma chère," she said, "*imagine-toi Maman* and *Papa* in the brilliance of the ballroom, leading a quadrille. Always, always the first on the floor." She sketched this romantic couple in the Illinois air. "Ev'ry eye upon *Maman en grande toilette* and *Papa* golden-hair and all in midnight black. You have not live until . . ." Her voice sighed to silence so I could see them for myself.

Then when I had, she turned full on me. Her eyes had darkened with the day. They glistened. What did I know of homesickness, who'd never been away from home? She spoke low. "You would destroy all that, all I come from, and know."

I didn't want to fight the war with her. For one thing, I thought I might lose.

I pulled away from her eyes and looked around for something else to say. "Cass is usually up here by now." I tried to think how to explain Cass.

"She is droll, that one," Delphine said.

"She sees things that ain't there."

"She has visions?" Delphine was interested at once. "She is a seeress?"

"I don't know about that," I said. "Mama's worried to death Cass will lose her mind."

"But it is a gift she has!" Delphine exclaimed.

"Not in these parts," I said, wondering what I'd blurt out next.

The river flows calmer at the end of the day for some reason. By and by we began to feel the evening chill. Delphine and I climbed down the Backbone to the house. On the porch stood a crate with the lamps and the oil.

"Eh, the lamp boy makes his escape." Delphine rolled her eyes. "He skedaddle before you find him."

I was flushed in cheek and neck, and silent for once.

"You are sweet on the lamp boy, isn't it so?" Delphine peered into my bonnet for the truth.

So it looked like she knew everything anyway, without you had to tell her.

But I was forgotten in the next moment. As quick as we were in the door of the house, another scent I'd never smelled wafted our way.

Delphine breathed deep and fell back, clutching her shawls. "Jambalaya!" she shrieked. "*Merci, bon Dieu,* we are save!"

How well I recall Delphine and me coming in from that damp evening, pulling off her bonnets. Calinda, treetop-tall, had her face to the fire and her skirts pinned up under an apron of Mama's. She was browning onions in the biggest skillet. Nearly stuck to her side was Cass, measuring paste out of a jar.

The kitchen was ranked with provisions Calinda and Delphine must have brought with them. A sack of rice and another of red beans. A wreath of onions, a coil of sausage, a mess of little bird's-eye peppers.

It was Calinda's fireside now, and I was astonished to see Mama setting at the kitchen table. She wasn't idle. She didn't know how to be idle. But daylight had never caught her setting down. She was into a sack of pecans we'd gathered out in the timber last fall. In a litter of shells she was picking out nutmeats.

She glanced up, a little shamed about her ease. I seemed to see for the first time how twisted and knobby her hands were. Winter got to her joints, and she had pain she never spoke of. Looked to me like she'd surrendered her kitchen without a skirmish.

And didn't we eat that night? Always before, pig's cheek in pot likker was a banquet to us, when we could get it. Now we ate our first jambalaya, thick with tomato paste and the sausage and a slab of salt ham we had, and alive with the onions—all poured over the snowy rice.

Real abolitionists wouldn't eat rice or cane sugar or anything the South produced. We dug right in. My insides didn't know which way to turn. Noah ate his fill too, twice. But he'd miss his mouth for stealing glances at Delphine. We saw now what a good appetite she enjoyed. She was always to be a hearty eater, though she couldn't boil water herself. She'd have starved to death in a well-stocked larder.

Calinda was back and forth from table to fire, but she ate her share. Life stirred in her dark eyes. How beautiful her long hands were, dishing up, feeding us. Cass was right there beside her, watching Calinda's hands, hearing her silences.

Night never come. We had the new coal oil lamps, you see. Once they were filled and we struck the matches and saw how the wicks worked, the kitchen sprang to life just as the hearth fire began to die.

We covered our mouths at the sight of one another, Mama and Cass and me. Somehow it was brighter than day, and we were players on the showboat stage. Light found all the corners. The crockery glared from the shelf. I looked at Noah and caught my breath. I swear I hadn't noticed before how handsome he was. We were twins. How come he got the looks?

He was dazed by the light, or Delphine. She'd summoned up her sewing from an elegant basket with seed pearls and tiny shells patterned on the lid. In her hands was a pair of ladies' underdrawers to be mended, though I didn't think Noah needed to be seeing them. She leaned into the lamplight as if it was nothing to her, and the silver thimble on her finger glimmered like a star.

Calinda brought forth a pack of playing cards, and laid them out on the table in the circle of light. Mama didn't hold with cards in the house. But she said nothing because Cass was transfixed, watching each card Calinda snapped down. Whether they were playing those cards or reading them, I couldn't tell. But much passed between them, and Mama was relieved to see Cass so bright-eyed.

How at home our visitors were, these light-bringers. How settled they seemed to be, not like birds of passage at all.

Chapter Six

Summer comes to Grand Tower in May. The leafed-out trees screen the view. Snakes hang in the green willow walls that sweep the river's edge. Cass and me had cut each other out of our winter underwear, and we were all barefoot, all but Delphine.

The windows of our house blazed with lamplight every night now. We'd have been a landmark, a lighthouse astride the Devil's Backbone. And the boats still came. We didn't know how quiet the first weeks of war can be. We had no experience of war.

The Southern boats ran low in the water with their burden of cotton bales. Even now, a few holdouts still believed that King Cotton might keep the peace. And most every New Orleans boat brought fresh provisions from Delphine's *maman.* Curry Marshall and Noah were forever lugging a trunk up the Backbone, another treasure chest from Madame Clemence Duval. Eats and coffee beans and a grinder, salts and powders and all manner of things you didn't know you needed.

Her *maman* sent up the hand mirror that Delphine had left behind. She'd been half crazy without it, and it drew me like a magnet. I'd never seen myself in a mirror before. I'd seen my reflection in a pan of water and even in the river, rippled. But me and Cass always fixed each other's hair. We didn't have a mirror in the house, though you'd catch a glimpse of yourself after dark in a windowpane. They must have had one down at Rodgers's store, but I don't remember it. Now I stole every look I could get at Delphine's mirror. It was gold, with violets painted on the back. I wasn't overencouraged by what I saw, but it made me so real. I'm not sure I knew that I existed and took up space of my own before I saw me in that mirror.

A summer wardrobe came for Delphine: dimities and lavender lawn, straw bonnets, embroidered chemises. And muslins and calicoes for Calinda. My head swam.

People naturally talked. What else was there to talk about but them Secesh gals, that Delphine and that Calinda? A rumor went round that Calinda was an escaped slave. And for giving her shelter, us Pruitts were being called Republicans. Before Fort Sumter, an escaped slave was apt to be sold back South. Now it was only talk, though why an escaped slave would bring her mistress with her nobody seemed to know.

Mama didn't like any kind of talk behind our back, even if it was hogwash. But all her thoughts were trained on Noah. He still drilled in the road. Every day she stayed him from war was a little victory. If Delphine was helping to keep him with us, so be it. Mama could just about put up with Noah moon-calfing around the place as long as he was there. She melted a little more on the day Delphine drew out of a New Orleans trunk the grandest dress I ever saw. When she held it up, it was far too long in the skirts for herself.

It was for Mama, a gift from Madame Duval. A bottle-green silk with a lace bertha and all the horsehair petticoats to go under. Mama naturally didn't want to take it. A gift was a little too close to charity to suit her. But I watched her close and knew she was seeing herself in that dress, and the woman she might have been. Delphine didn't reason with her long before Mama caved in. Still, it was too fine for her to touch. "Tilly," she told me, "take it up to the death drawer."

Like everybody else, we had us a sick drawer and a death drawer in a bureau along the upstairs hall. The sick drawer held our remedies. The death drawer kept a supply of winding-sheets and a selection of garments for when the time come. Mama meant she'd be buried in this dress. You ought to have seen the look on Delphine's face.

I suppose it give Mama comfort to know that she'd be laid out in such elegant raiment. In the long run, she was never to wear it at all. Nobody did.

It's up there in the death drawer yet.

While Delphine would starve in a pantry, Calinda would thrive in a wilderness, and did. I think she only went up to the devil's footstool to mope with Cass once. Ever after she saw to it that they were out in the timber, looking for whatever might be useful: horehound leaves and lady slipper and wild strawberries. At the big spring, they found watercress, and Calinda made us salads out of it, which we weren't used to.

She went into business, meeting every steamboat that stopped. Down the Backbone she'd stride in fresh aprons and her best bandannas—"tignons," as Delphine said they were called. Heaped high on a tray slung around her neck were her own pecan pralines, each candy done up in a paper frill. Our kitchen was a swamp of seething sugar and bubbling molasses. Calinda boiled up and dropped out pralines pretty nearly around the clock. Cass rose out of her trundle at daybreak to build up the fire.

Grand Tower came to expect Calinda passing in her big-tailed tignon. Her who never raised her voice stood at the foot of the gangplank and sang out, "PRAWLEEENS, NEW ORLEANS STYLE." And they were very shortly pounding down the plank to get at them, passengers and crew alike.

Cass hung back in public, but Calinda needed her to fetch and carry. Cass was soon down there with her, handing over the pralines while Calinda caught the money in her apron.

Oh, that first day when she dumped all them coins onto the kitchen table! I wanted to bar the door. In the end, we took to putting all the money they brought home in a tin can and hung it down the well.

I was to remember that spring as a golden time. It was wicked to think so. People were dying already. St. Louis blew sky-high on the tenth day of May. But we had light at our windows and talk at the table; we'd never et so good, there was ready money down the well, and we still had Noah.

Cass didn't find the time to mope and mourn now she had Calinda. Calinda was the sister Cass needed. I'd hugged her to me and wiped her nose. But she needed what I couldn't give. Her and Calinda spoke a language I was deaf to, a language of prophecies and cures, of visions and the medicines waiting out in the timber to heal the afflicted. They spoke in tongues foreign to me, even when they weren't speaking at all. And so I was sorry Cass had slipped away from my smothering arms, but glad in my heart she'd joined the living.

We sat through our glowing evenings, listening to Delphine's stories of New Orleans life, though very little of her own. We brought our chores closer to hear her tales. And like the girl in *Arabian Nights,* she never run dry. Cass listened too while she watched Calinda lay out the cards at her end of the table.

Each day came to the same end. After whole evenings of silence, Calinda would sweep up her cards and announce, *"Mo kalle dodo."*

It didn't even sound like Delphine's French. But it seemed to mean she was going to bed. Calinda was a creature of few words and, I suppose, an example to us all.

Throughout our evenings, Noah never ran short of excuses to hover nearby. He turned cobbler to repair Delphine's slippers because their heels were forever coming off. He hunkered on the hearth with nails in his mouth, and Delphine spun her yarns to the tap of his hammer. Though I was never to be a needlewoman, I darned Noah's socks over an egg, and made a place for myself in the circle of lamplight. I caught a glimpse of happiness, and saw it was a bird on a branch, fixing to take wing.

The St. Louis news was all bad. The governor of Missouri had told Jeff Davis he'd better send help if he wanted another star in the Confederate flag. It was rumored that a boat come up from Baton Rouge, loaded with rifles. The Missouri militias were all for the South; the St. Louis militias were German and solid for the North. They clashed over the arsenal, and twenty-eight were killed.

Lightning struck that close, north of where we were. I naturally thought of Delphine's St. Louis aunt, Madame

LeBlanc. I wondered if, as Delphine would say, "she was murder in her bed." But Mama didn't like war talk in the house, and Delphine made no murmur of her aunt. Did I begin to wonder if Madame LeBlanc had ever existed at all?

But I tried not to look ahead, and so it was a golden time. And when it began to unravel the way things do, I had warning.

In the deepest part of the night, I came awake to see the trundle empty and Cass over on the windowsill. Her face was silvery wet with moonlight. She stared at what wasn't there, and I saw in her slump that it was the old Cass come back, Cass having a fearful vision.

She was so silent that I don't know what woke me. But she was bent in agony. One hand clutched the other arm, and she rocked back and forth, gray with pain.

I didn't go to her, God help me. I feared too much what she felt. I couldn't help her, and I didn't want to know. I must have slept again, but I'd known a warning when I saw one.

Only a day or so later Delphine and I were coming back up past the chicken yard from the privy when we seen a small parcel on the porch.

We never went near the woodshed in summer and we never went alone to the privy because of the snakes. It was hard to keep the weeds down, and there was that old story about the country woman in her privy who was bit from below by a cottonmouth. It was one of them stories that never dies out, like Mrs. Champ Hazelrigg being et by her hogs. We always went to the privy in pairs, and one of us carried the hoe.

Delphine saw it first, a rag tied up in a bundle just where Curry Marshall had left the lamps. We dropped down on the porch stairs while I worked the knot, my mind a blank. There was nothing inside but a rock to make weight, two red ribbons lettered in gold, and a note folded up tight.

The ribbons were the prizes Curry Marshall had won for spelling at the bees years back at school, so the note was meant for me. Delphine knew by watching my face as I smoothed out the paper.

I'd never had a letter in my life, and precious few words from Curry Marshall's mouth.

Dear Tilly,

As your eyes scan this page, I am away with Mose and Jaret to Williamson County to join up with the good fellows there mustering under Thorndike Brooks and Harvey Hayes. We march south to Paducah or wherever we can find us a Confederate militia to soldier with.

Now that Captain Grant has organized a Northern regiment at Anna, Egypt's no place for them of my convictions. If I had me a pocket watch or anything of value, I would leave it in your safekeeping. Here find within my spelling ribbons instead.

They say that all the best oficers that ever come out of West

Point are on the Secesh side. I expect we'll have it over by Christmas.

May this find you as it leaves me,

Yours very truly,

C. Marshall

I read it through twice. If Curry could spell *officers,* he might have won blue ribbons instead of red. His letter chilled me, and stirred me up. My eyes didn't sting or moisten, but I felt like a turned-out glove. Delphine noticed.

"'Tain't a love letter," I told her. "Nothing like that."

Delphine gave one of her little shrugs. She wore fewer petticoats in this weather, and Calinda was too busy now to give her hair more than a lick and a promise. "A soldier must leave someone behind," she said. "What men do best is walk away from women. Wars are handy for that."

This seemed so worldly-wise I wondered if she could be nineteen.

"Curry says it's all apt to be over by Christmas."

Delphine shrugged that off too. "Wars are always to be over by Christmas. At least he fights on the side of right."

"But if Curry wins, Noah loses." Did it cross my mind they could both lose?

A quiet moment followed. There weren't many quiet moments in Delphine's vicinity, but now you could hear voices from town, and the river lapping the bank. We sat there with our skirttails tucked under us. At last she said,

"You are relieve it is the lamp boy who goes, and not Noah."

She read my heart aright. It was one of her talents. Sorry though I was to see Curry go, I could have burst into song right where we set that it wasn't Noah going. Not yet.

Somehow my heart could spare Curry. If war had never come—if Delphine had never come—it might have been different. But war took Curry away. And Delphine made me begin to look around myself, and farther from myself. I didn't know what to make of that great world she come from, but she made me want more in my small one. And so Curry and me wasn't to be.

It's as well I could spare him, because I never heard from him or of him again. People could vanish without a trace in them times, and you dreaded the next one who might.

They said that on the morning Curry's mother found him gone, she went to the timber and howled like a wolf with her grief and her fear. I thought of Mama.

Then in the middle of May, with Missouri turning on itself across the river, the blockade was enforced. The boats no longer ran between here and New Orleans, and so there was no turning back for Delphine and Calinda. I wondered what they thought about that, but Delphine would tell you exactly what she wanted you to hear, and Calinda didn't even tell that much.

I thought an empty river would put her out of the praline business. But the boats still ran on the upper Mississippi, as far down as Cairo and up the Ohio River to Louisville that had decided to be neutral. So we got some boats, though fewer than before. Calinda met them all, calling out now, "LAST CHANCE FOR PRAWLEEENS, NEW ORLEANS STYLE." As the summer deepened, our kitchen was still hot as hinges with boiling sugar.

I well remember once when we heard a boat was coming down from Davenport. It must have been a Monday because Delphine and me were in the yard, and I was at the laundry tub. Though she could sew a fine seam, she did very little other work. Even on laundry day, she only sorted.

As I stirred our boiling clothes with my skirts hiked to keep them out of the fire, we heard the boat's whistle. Out of the house flounced Calinda with a mound of pralines on her tray. Right behind her come Cass, just as ready for business. Cass's wispy hair was tied up in one of Calinda's tignons. It made me smile to see Cass switching her skirts down the stairs like a scrawny, pale reflection of Calinda, including the tignon, tied in a tidy knot.

But the minute Delphine saw, she made a run for them. Quicker than thought, she snatched the tignon off Cass's head. Cass jumped a foot and shrank. Delphine turned on Calinda and shook the tignon in her face. I was glad not to hear what she said. When she pointed back to the laundry pot, I took it to mean that if Calinda let Cass wrap a tignon around her head again, Delphine would personally put it on the fire.

She won the battle, and the other two scurried off down the hill about their business, though Cass looked back in case Delphine was after them. Then she returned to her sorting. I pondered this, though I wasn't surprised she had a temper.

Was the tignon a sign and proof of slavery that would shame Cass, that scrawny scrap of white humanity? We'd seen pictures of slave women with their heads tied up in kerchiefs, like Calinda's, though not so elegant.

But Delphine, eyes still crackling, snapped across the laundry pot at me, "She has not earned the tignon, your sister!"

And what that could mean, I couldn't think.

Summer began to hang heavy. The garden wilted, and Cass's chickens drooped in whatever shade they could find. Every hot morning I couldn't draw breath until I saw Noah was still there. We heard the army was full of fifteen-year-old boys. They'd lied to get in, and the militias had pretended to believe them.

Then came the third week of July, and word from Manassas of the first big battle of the war, the Battle of Bull Run. It was off in the state of Virginia, but in this first great clash between North and South, the South had won.

People stared openmouthed at the Cairo newspaper pinned up at the landing, struck dumb by what we read. When our soldiers come up against General Jackson and his First Virginia, the "Stonewall Brigade," our boys cut and run.

We read how the women of Washington had ridden out that Sunday morning in high-wheeled buggies, with parasols and picnic hampers to watch the North finish off the South in a single skirmish. The women fled in a panic back to Washington, and running ahead of them were our soldiers, "all sense of manhood forgotten," according to the Cairo paper.

We didn't know what to think. It turned our world around. But from that day forth, all Egypt and Grand Tower for sure were solid for the North. The first boys who'd marched off in April to answer President Lincoln's call had been stoned in the road by the Democrats. But the Battle of Bull Run made Yankees out of us all because it was going to take every one of us to win it. The flag seemed to wave from every house, even from the doctor's office, though people said Dr. Hutchings was a peacemaker.

You'd have thought that being on the same side would have encouraged people to pull together. But people aren't made that way.

Chapter Seven

Delphine always made time for her trips down to Front Street, to take the air, as she said. She'd come to terms with Rodgers's store, since that's all we had to offer, and gave it a light browsing most afternoons. Like Calinda, she became a landmark. Grand Tower had never seen anything like either of these beings, though as it turned out, Delphine stirred them more.

Once she reached flat ground, she moved with wondrous grace, under a parasol hanging in points of lacework. The word went round that she never wore the same bonnet twice. This brought every woman in town to the window, to see her passing by. She had, in fact, five or six bonnets, including the new straw ones. But she retrimmed them throughout the evenings from a bottomless supply of artificial flowers and fruit, grosgrain rosettes, glittering buckles, and feathers Calinda brought from the timber.

Front Street was a loblolly down by the landing, and so Delphine had to gather her skirts to keep them clear of the mud. This brought every loafer in Jackson County to the porch of T. W. Jenkins's store, hoping for a glimpse of her ankles. Until the last showboat played Grand Tower that summer, Delphine was the greatest draw in this part of the state. And this Secesh gal strolled a town that was snapping with the Stars and Stripes of Union flags.

She hadn't been gone long when I noticed a knot of women down in the distance one afternoon. They were starting up our hill. Cass and Calinda had taken a dip net down to the river, so I was the only one who saw. I was beating the braided rugs over the porch railing.

I'd heard somewheres of ladies with no more to do than call on one another in the afternoons. That didn't sound much like Grand Tower. And the climb alone would have discouraged them from us. Still, here a bunch came, looking for more pathway than they could find.

Darting inside, I told Mama. I didn't see surprise in her face. But she grabbed her head to smooth her hair and sent me for her shoes. She'd cast off her apron for a fresh one by the time I got back. She was still cramming her bare feet into the shoes when we heard them on the porch.

One of them was Mrs. T. W. Jenkins. Another was Mrs. Manfred Cady. And Mrs. R. M. Breeze, the preacher's wife.

They looked like three of Cass's hens, all feathered out but suffering in this heat. They were sucking air to catch their breath.

Mama pretended surprise to see them, as if she spent a summer day in her shoes and a fresh apron.

"Mrs. Pruitt," Mrs. Manfred Cady said, "it is hot weather and a hard climb, and we are all busy women, preparin' for war."

She fetched up a shuddering breath, and Mama said, calmly, "I am up for the day myself."

"We won't take more than a moment of your time," Mrs. Jenkins said, and in they came, looking around as they'd never set foot here before.

Mama could have shown them into the front room for a breath of air from the river. She gestured them into chairs around the table. The kitchen hung in the foreign scent of Calinda's *pain-patate,* a New Orleans gingerbread, baking in the Dutch oven. The whole kitchen was an oven. Mrs. Breeze sighed.

"Mrs. Pruitt, we all understand that life has not been an easy row for you to hoe," said Mrs. Cady.

Mama's hands were folded before her. "I haven't asked for charity in this town." Her gaze brushed Mrs. Breeze. "What good would it do me?"

"Nobody mentioned charity," Mrs. Cady went on, "and it's nobody's business but your own who you let out your rooms to or who you take under your roof."

Mama clearly saw eye-to-eye with her on that.

"But the tide has turned, Mrs. Pruitt," said Mrs. Cady. "Now our watchword must be 'United We Stand, Divided We Fall.' I will put it plain. We are at war, in case you haven't heard, and you've got enemy aliens in your house. We come in good faith to let you know you're on thin ice."

"And you're givin' them succor," Mrs. Breeze chimed.

Mama's hands clenched in her apron. But she spoke mildly. "Well, I don't see how I can send them home. The boats isn't running."

She glanced at the preacher's wife. We weren't churchgoers. For one thing, we'd never had the clothes. Mrs. Breeze had been agog since she got here, to see how heathens lived. "Shall I send them down to the preacher for shelter?" Mama inquired.

Mrs. Breeze bristled. "I wouldn't have them at the parsonage overnight," she said, about to spit. "I wouldn't give them loft space in the barn, nor straw from the stable. We're true-blue Americans here, and the whole community knows what they are."

Mama's eyes narrowed. "What are they?"

"Why, spies, of course," Mrs. Cady rang out. "One of them's eternally out in the timber, surveyin' the territory for an invasion, they say. And the white one's all over town, gettin' the lay of the land. She's down there right now."

"Spies." Mama pondered. "Then they come to the wrong town, didn't they? If we had a secret, you three would tell it."

The bonnets quivered and drew closer. They hadn't made that climb to be insulted.

"And another thing," Mrs. T. W. Jenkins piped up. "It's enough to gag a maggot to see that overdressed little miss, that Delphine whoever, putting herself on public display. She's switchin' her skirttails up and down Front Street even as we speak. And the men in this town is starin' holes in her, the brazen little hussy."

Mama stroked her cheek. "She's a big-city gal," Mama said at last. "She don't know how restless small-town men can get. They say the porch on your husband's store is about to collapse under the weight of the men watching Delphine go by. I can see how it might be a worry to you."

Mrs. Jenkins jumped on that. "If you're insinuatin' my husband has any interest in that painted-up little floozy, I have only this in answer to you, Mrs. Pruitt. I've held on to my husband, unlike some I could name."

The kitchen went dead. You could hear the buzz of a horsefly circling.

Then Mama said, "Get out of my house."

They'd never been ordered out of anywhere. They bumbled and bumped into one another. Mrs. Cady gave Mrs. Jenkins a look like maybe she'd gone too far. They were at the door when the preacher's wife turned back.

"Mrs. Pruitt," she said, speaking low, "as one mother to another, I will have to say my piece. It don't look good, havin' a son the age of your boy under the same roof with young women we don't know nothin' about, spies or otherwise. It just don't look right."

I was next to Mama, standing with her. "I don't reckon my son will be under my roof much longer," Mama said. "You have a son, don't you? Will he be going to war?"

"My son? Bertram?" Mrs. Breeze stared. "My land, no, he won't be goin' to war. He's fort—thirt—why, no, he won't be goin'."

Then they were gone.

Mama leaned against the doorjamb where we lingered for the air. She smoothed her apron and thought about taking it off to spare it. Then at length she spoke, softly. "I work hard not to draw their fire, and to keep us decent and together. I live and let live. I don't even go down to town if I can send one of you. But it don't signify. They can't let you be. One day they come after you."

That was a long speech for Mama. Now in the quiet I was thinking about Paw, and wondered if she was too. But we rarely spoke of him, and didn't now.

"What'll happen next, Mama?"

She stroked her chin. "Well, they wouldn't dare to run Delphine out of town. It wouldn't look good to their menfolk. I have an idea they've got it out of their systems."

"Mama, do you wish Delphine and Calinda had never come? Would it just have been easier on us to be like we was?"

She looked over at me in surprise. I was as tall as she was now. "No, I'm not sorry they come. You can't believe but every other word Delphine says. And if vanity's a sin, she'll fry. But before she got here, I wouldn't have answered back to them battleaxes. That Delphine don't lack confidence in herself. I'll give her that. I believe a little has wore off on me. She put some starch in my spine."

I hadn't thought of such a thing. I didn't know grown people changed, or were changed. I thought being grown was safer than that.

"Delphine's wearing off on you too," Mama told me, "just like Calinda's wearing off on Cass."

"Delphine? On me?"

"It's in your walk, a little. And you're tidier about your hair. You don't look so much like you was dragged backwards through a brush-fence."

"Many thanks, Mama," I said. "But not the corsets. Never them."

"Well, no," Mama said. "There's limits."

Then not two minutes after our recent callers had vanished from view, there came Delphine toiling up toward us.

Climbing the Backbone was the biggest job of her day. Her summer dress was made of ticking, a fine black line against white. She had it in handfuls, climbing over rill and ridge. She labored along like she could feel every stone through her thin slipper soles. The silken morning glories on her bonnet looked to be working loose. Her face was beet red and streaming in this heat, and her curls hung lank. She was using the parasol for a walking stick.

It was a far cry from strolling the pavements of New Orleans, but she kept true to her ways. I glanced at Mama. She was stifling a smile at the sight of all this elegance melting away. And it took something to coax a smile out of Mama.

Delphine fetched up at the bottom of the porch stairs, breathing so heavy you'd think she'd been pulling stumps. *"Nom de Dieu,"* she gasped, and several other French words.

Planting the parasol in the ground, she plunged a gloved hand into her reticule. Yes, gloves in this weather, little string ones with her bare fingers sticking out. She pulled up a handbill and shook it at us.

"A showboat! It comes down from somewhere called Muscatine, Iowa. But of course the musicians are from New Orleans, where else? The Ethiopian Melodiers. And a drama! And the E. P. Christy minstrels! And 'the public is invited to dance upon the stage at the conclusion of the program!'" she quoted. "A showboat, and the last before they are taken off the river!"

Delphine was almost beside herself. Mama and I saw then how dull her life had been all this time she was making it so lively for us.

So of course when the showboat played Grand Tower, we'd go. Mama too. Our visitors that afternoon had something to do with it. Then Noah dispelled all doubt in the matter.

He came home from his work that night, lips white with anger. Being Noah, he'd have said nothing, though I heard him kick at the porch stairs before I saw him. My spine was starchier than before too, so I trailed him into his room. There I demanded to know what particular burr had got under his saddle.

He didn't want to tell, and then he did. "They run their mouths down there around the forge," he said, disgusted with humanity. "They talk to hear their heads rattle. I'd like to shorten the ears off about six of them. Maybe more."

"What for?"

"They say we're sending signals to the South from the light out of our windows."

"Who?"

"Us," he snapped. "They say we're signaling the Confederate Navy out of this house. It's what the lamps is for."

He was wrought up for certain.

"This is talk against Delphine," I said. "They mean Delphine's spying."

Of course that's just what they meant, like there was any sense to it. Men gossip worse than women and don't even know it.

Noah was hopping mad. As if trying to court a girl under his own roof didn't give him fits enough. For one thing, he wouldn't own up to how sweet he was on Delphine. For another, there was always witnesses to every little thing. The wonder is Noah didn't flee this house of women sooner than he did.

I let him rant, and use some language I won't repeat here. It wasn't like him. But we'd be going to the showboat show. No question about that. We'd pull the money out of the well for the tickets, and we'd all sit on the front row like anybody else. Maybe more so.

Chapter Eight

Delphine, who didn't know she was a spy, spent feverish days planning for the night of the show. It was a great event, the last of the showboats before they were all turned into hospital ships for the soldiers, or gunboats. But, my, how she fussed, turning out her trunks for finery.

On an August day hot enough to pop the corn in their rows, we heard that the showboat had cleared Cape Girardeau and was making for us. Delphine napped that afternoon. "Beauty sleep," Mama remarked.

Calinda had said, "Me, I stay at 'ome." But Delphine wouldn't hear of it. *Mais non,* Calinda had to go because it was going to be a *gran de boubousse* and not to be missed. And who knows, maybe Calinda wanted to go all along. With her you never knew. She put a pot of her gumbo 'zerbe at the back of the fire for our quick supper. We weren't hungry, but Noah had to eat.

When Delphine summoned Calinda upstairs, Cass went too. While they were up there, I pictured Cass and Calinda with a foot apiece in the small of Delphine's back, yanking on her corset strings.

Then by and by Mama and me looked up from our work to see a stranger in the hall door. A perfect stranger. I jumped. It was a young lady, slender as a willow wand, her hair puffed over her little shell-pink ears. She wore a sprigged dimity with a froth of lace at the throat. Her rosebud lips were a good deal pinker than her ears. Her dark-fringed eyes were cast modestly down. She looked up at us. It was Cass.

Mama dropped whatever was in her hands. My jaw was on the floor. "Cassy?" I said.

Wet-eyed, Mama whispered, "Girl, what have they did to you?" But she couldn't take her eyes off Cass. I couldn't either.

I wanted to make a run for her, but hugging had never worked. Now she was made of dainty china, too perfect to touch. But it was still Cass. She went shy after the first moment.

When I could look away from her, I saw in Mama something new, something of joy, even hope. Just a flicker. But she nudged me and said, "You better skin upstairs and see what they can do with you."

Heaven help me, I went up there. On the table that Delphine called her *secrétaire,* where she wrote letters to her *maman,* I saw a fearful sight. It was a blazing coal oil lamp. On the glass chimney rested a curling iron, heating up. Delphine and Calinda, in states of undress, turned on me.

"Oh no," says I, "not the curling iron! You won't get red-hot metal that close to my head."

But they did. I was a lamb unto the slaughter as they worked me over, giving me curls fried like Delphine's to frame my face. They jerked me into a dress of hers. I could wear it without corsets, so little figure did I have. It was a transformation that cost me dear. I felt frizzled and scalped at the end of it, and hobbled by petticoats.

They showed me beautiful tall tortoiseshell combs with glints of diamond in them. "I can't wear them things," I said. "My head ain't big enough to carry them."

"For your *maman,*" said Delphine.

In the distance a showboat's whistle split the afternoon. *"Écoutez donc,"* she cried. "Hear that!" Her eyes flashed black fire because a steam calliope was playing "Annie Laurie." The melody drifted over the water to us. We knew that song, parts of it, so we began to sing:

Her brow is like the snow-drift,
Her throat is like the swan,
Her face is the fair-est
That e'er the sun shone on.

We sang and danced around their room, Delphine and me, while Calinda looked on, almost smiling at us jumping over the clutter of this sudden ballroom floor.

It might be the last show we'd ever see, so they come from all over to see it. All Grand Tower was there, except for the preacher and Mrs. Breeze. They come from Makanda, and people rowed over from the Missouri side. We sat on the front row of skittery gold chairs. Noah Pruitt, hair slicked, in his paw's coat, sat by his womenfolk as the town had not seen us before, and never would again.

Mama hadn't unearthed the green silk from the death drawer, but she wore her otherwise best. And a black velvet ribbon that Calinda had tied around her neck. Deft hands had drawn Mama's hair out of its knot and dressed it high with the Spanish combs that struck sparks in the light. Behind us the room buzzed, and for once she didn't give a hoot what they might be saying.

I'd never been on a boat of any sort, so I didn't know what to expect. We sat in a great satin-lined, tufted candy box, glowing like high noon under the chattering chandeliers. It was exactly what I hoped the world would be—this bright, with gold dust in the air, and throbbing with music.

The Melodiers were on the stage, playing their fiddles and drums and horns. They played the audience in with songs they'd gathered from all the rivers they'd traveled: "Come Where My Love Lies Dreaming" and "Oh! Susanna" and "Drowned Maiden's Hair" and "Old Dan Tucker."

A drama came next, a play, and I'd never seen one. We were promised it had never been given before and was written in the light of recent events.

Abe Lincoln strode onto the stage.

The audience gasped. But it wasn't the real Abe Lincoln. It was a tall galoot with side-whiskers like his. In the play he wasn't exactly the President of the United States. He was the father of two daughters, though in real life, as we all knew, he only had sons. But they were such pretty girls, though painted up like Delphine. With the prettiest dresses.

As I'd never seen a play, it was hard to follow. But one of the sisters was dutiful. I understood that. The other one was headstrong and seemed not to have a brain in her head. It took me most of the play to decide that the dutiful daughter represented the Union and the other one who wouldn't listen was the Confederacy. So there was the Yankee daughter and her Secesh sister.

The play went on at some length with argument and weeping. But I can quote Abe Lincoln's last lines to this day:

Go then, our rash sister!
Afar and aloof—
Run wild in the sunshine
Away from our roof,
But when your heart aches
And your feet have grown sore,
Remember the pathway
That leads to our door!

The curtain dropped. The band struck up "The Battle Hymn of the Republic," and an American flag unfurled from the ceiling.

Applause rocked the boat, though Delphine beside me was disgusted by the whole thing. *"C'est incroyable,"* she muttered, and more, all in French. She fiddled with her feather fan. Beside her Calinda stared into space with her hands in her lap, so I suppose Cass did the same.

That was the serious part of the program. When the curtain rose again, it was a minstrel show with a line of men in chairs. The orchestra was black men. But the minstrels were white men who'd rubbed burnt cork on their faces to look black. You could see the white skin behind their ears.

The man at one end was called Mr. Bones. The man at the other end was Mr. Tambo. And the man in the middle was the Interlocutor, whatever that might be. This was the comic part, and they swapped a lot of jokes I didn't get. But the crowd roared. And they sang comic songs, like,

Mary had a little lamb.
With her it used to frolic.
It licked her cheek in play one day
And died of painter's colic.

Mary had a little lamb.
Her father killed it dead,
And now it goes to school with her
Between two hunks of bread.

When they rung down the curtain, I don't know that Delphine liked that part any better than the drama. She fanned fitfully and plucked at her skirts. Because of the corsets, you could hear her breathing.

The next time the curtain went up, the stage was bare. The audience was invited to come up and dance. It reminded me that we'd had a dance in town on the night Delphine and Calinda had first come here. The orchestra struck up a lively tune, a cakewalk called "Little Alligator Bait."

People hung back. It wasn't our kind of dancing. It wasn't a square dance called by Mr. Chilly Attabury. But couples edged onto the stage. Then in this night of wonders, Noah was bowing over Delphine, putting out his hand for all our world to see. My land, he was handsome, though defiant around the eyes. Delphine pressed her feather fan against her bosom and cast great fringed eyes up at him. He was asking her to dance, and it was a waltz. She held back only a short while.

"Mama," I muttered, "does Noah know how to do that kind of dancing?"

"We're fixing to find out," she replied.

The stage was half full of couples waltzing, or trying to. But when Noah led Delphine onto the floor, all eyes were upon them. Her hoopskirts were wide enough to drive every other woman off the stage and overboard. Her shawl was filmy net, the evening being hot as day. Her black dress was cut low to show the curve of her plump shoulders. A bouquet of artificial cabbage roses bloomed on her breast. When she reached high to plant her little mitted hand on Noah's shoulder, she engulfed him with her feather fan. And away they waltzed, her leading.

It was a sight to behold, and everybody beheld it. Behind us, the same women who'd resented Delphine's bonnets stood now to study the drape of her skirts. The men were all standing up too, bug-eyed. They saw the Confederate spy bewitching the local boy. And given half a chance, Noah would have shortened the ears of any man who called him on it.

Wonder followed wonder. A shadow fell o'er me, and there was Dr. William Hutchings, bowing. I'd never been near him. And he was old. He was twenty-five if he was a minute. He put out his hand. Delphine had hesitated prettily. I shrank. He looked to Mama. "Mrs. Pruitt, might I have the honor of a waltz with your daughter?"

Mama said he could have me, and he led me in a trance up on the stage. His coat was swallow-tailed, and the points of his high collar bit into his beard. "That's a mighty pretty dress you're wearing, Miss Pruitt," he remarked.

"Well, it's Delphine's," I explained, every curl aquiver, "and I don't know as I can waltz."

It was a right pretty dress, yellowish tussore with ribbons run through.

"If you find the waltz is beyond you," Dr. Hutchings said, "you need only climb onto my boots, and I will do the steps for us both."

This was so odd a notion that I forgot my fears and settled into the doctor's arms. I found I could waltz, if only for that evening, though I clumped some in my winter shoes. But Dr. Hutchings was an expert dancer. Being along in years, he'd no doubt had much practice. We turned in the dazzle of light, and the petticoats rushed round my ankles. I was pretty nearly some other girl entirely.

But waltzing is work, especially in this climate. Even Delphine, who never minded the limelight, seemed ready to rest when we were returned to our chairs. She was flushed, though whether from the dance or the nearness of Noah her eyes didn't say.

Then everything changed.

One of the black men, the fiddler, crept to the edge of the stage and peered down at our row. He pointed his bow and called out, "Calinda!"

It silenced the room. Delphine, who sat between us, was motionless. Calinda stuck out her chin at the fiddler and then looked away.

"Danse, Calinda, bou-djoumb! Bou-djoumb!"

Calinda shrugged him off, and my heart thumped. It was as if something had come up the river to claim her. I didn't know whether to fear for her or not.

"Allons danser, Calinda," the man said, seeming to plead with her.

C'est pas tout le monde qui connaît
Danser les danses du vieux temps,

he sang.

Delphine murmured what he was singing, though she never looked my way:

It is not everyone who knows
How to dance the old-time dances.

The room held its breath when Calinda rose at last from her chair. She glided straight-backed to the steps and onto the stage, her face a grave mask. Her tignon was patterned in palm leaves. Her skirts were three layers of gauzy indienne, each a different color. Of course she was a dancer. Why hadn't I seen it the first time I ever laid eyes on her? She was a dancer in every step, every turn of her head.

The Melodiers struck up, and the strange, quick music tugged at her skirttails. Her beautiful hands came up to grab the air. She held back from the song, then plunged into it:

Allons danse Calinda
Danser collés Calinda,
Allons danse Calinda,
Pour faire fâcher les vielles femmes,

the bandsmen sang.

Delphine, whose fan moved in time with the music now, chanted:

Let's dance the Calinda,
Dance the Calinda close together,

Let's dance the Calinda
To make the old ladies mad.

The music quickened, and Calinda writhed like a sack of serpents. But her face was sober as Noah's, and her eyes elsewhere. Them who'd stood up to watch Delphine stood on their chairs now, to see Calinda's thrashing skirts, her bare feet drumming the floorboards. There may have been some who covered their eyes at this wild and wanton dance, but they were behind me and I didn't see.

I thought I'd pass out from the surprise of it, and the music that took you by the throat. Mama was a statue beside me. The audience began to keep time by clapping. Delphine fanned faster and swayed in her seat, a mirror reflecting Calinda's every move. When Calinda's head began to revolve to the music, so did Delphine's. They were both being called back by the mysterious place where they'd begun. I seemed to smell all the scents that traveled in their trunks, the spice and sweetgrass, the coffee and damp.

At last overcome, Delphine sprang out of her chair. She rushed to the edge of the stage, where Calinda was throwing her skirts, awash in the music.

"*Danse,* CoinCoin!" Delphine cried out, not herself at all. *"Danse!"* she shrieked, pounding the stage with her fist.

It might have gone on till morning. The song had no beginning and no end. But Calinda had danced herself into a frenzy. Her face was wet, and I saw she was crying. I didn't know she could. She plunged down the steps and up the aisle past the astonished crowd and away up the hill home.

Cass would have cut out after her, but Mama caught her. Delphine turned back blind from the edge of the stage. The black on her eyelashes ran in lines down her face. I saw then just how far from home she was.

The song shuddered to a stop, and the Melodiers carried their instruments off the stage. Delphine collapsed into her chair. She dropped her head on my shoulder for a moment while the muttering crowd filed out behind us.

"The fiddler knew her," I said.

"All New Orleans know her."

Delphine was recovering, reclaiming herself. "You have not live until you see her at the balls, on Wednesday nights, you know. Her and twenty or thirty like her, in the tignon, you see, and the skirts. You have not live until you see them dance the Calinda. It is a famous song, from the islands where . . ." She tapered off and closed a door in her mind.

"Her real name isn't Calinda?" I said into the silence. Mama and Cass and Noah listened.

"Mais non, chère," Delphine said absently. "She is called that because no one dances to the song as well. No one like my CoinCoin. All New Orleans is there to regard the spectacle. Ev'ry man. She is CoinCoin, an ancient name, older than the islands, back, back before . . ."

Another door closed inside her. She shut her fan and said no more.

If life was a storybook, that would have been the night Noah left us for the war. From the showboat stage, his face aglow in the footlights, he'd as good as announced his love to Grand Tower. He had someone to leave behind him when he went.

But he stayed on till the eve of our sixteenth birthday in September. I hated the birthday we shared from that day forward. He went as the other boys did, in the night to spare us good-byes. "Like a thief in the night," Mama said, trying in vain for bitterness to keep her heart from breaking.

Her eyes lost their faint glint of hope and went dead. They only sparked again when I did my poor best to comfort her. Though we rarely touched, I put my hand on her arm then for however that might help. But she jerked herself away as if my touch had burned her. I had nothing she wanted. She wanted Noah.

But he was gone from us, and the time the showboat come was a bright dream I must have had before the world went dark.

Chapter Nine

Noah was no hand to write, though better than I'd feared. But the days between his letters were long and shapeless. Then a scrawl of pencil stub on torn paper would come in a used envelope turned inside-out. Mama wouldn't touch it. But she couldn't do anything else until she heard me read it out to us all while she stared away at nothing, straining at the bit to see his face.

He'd joined the Thirty-first Illinois Infantry Regiment, organized after the awful defeat at Bull Run. He wrote a soldier's letters from up by Jacksonville, at Camp Dunlap. I squinted to find my brother between the lines. He was a little boastful at first for what he'd done, a little proud of not having a bath since he'd left home. Pleased with himself for not getting the trots when half the camp was down sick. "Beans'll kill more of us than bullets," he wrote.

At this first hint of dysentery in the camp, Calinda went to work, pouring her blackberry cordial cure for the runs into every bottle she could find a cork for. It was like her to see the truth behind Noah's letters before the rest of us.

They issued them no weapons up at Camp Dunlap, and no uniforms either. Noah wrote to say the legs of his butternut jeans were growing beards. They were given rations of salt pork and dry beans to cook for themselves if they could, or eat raw. That and thirteen dollars a month was their pay.

It was an army that didn't know how to be an army, and it treated its soldiers like beasts of the field.

"Men and boys, lost in a pasture!" Delphine said, shrugging elaborately at the helplessness of the other sex, and maybe Yankees.

Even after the first frost, the boys were still living outdoors, no canvas to sleep under, no blankets between them and the ground. We didn't have blankets, but we bundled up our patchwork quilts. Then when we were wondering how to send them off, we heard the Thirty-first had been ordered down to Cairo, to Camp Defiance.

I'd have kept that news from Mama if I could. She'd come to terms with Noah soldiering up by Jacksonville, farther from the South than we were ourselves. But everybody said that our war, the war on the river, would be waged from Cairo. In our ignorance we still couldn't believe they'd send boys unprepared into battle, though I suppose Cass knew better, in the way she knew things.

Two terrible weeks followed without a line from Noah. But we had word from Cairo. When Dr. Hutchings learned there weren't enough army doctors to go around, he shut up his Grand Tower office and went down there on his own.

The accounts he sent back were posted by the landing. All Grand Tower read them because the Thirty-first was an Egyptian regiment, made up of our boys.

Dr. Hutchings reported that half the Thirty-first were down with measles, and the other half were drunk. Cairo had shut its saloons and was anxious for battle to begin to get the soldiers off their streets and out of their gutters.

Delphine and I read the doctor's words and resolved to keep them from Mama. But somehow she knew.

It was October now with the days dwindling around us. I'd become a fitful sleeper, staring at the dark ceiling half the night, listening to Cass's soft snore from the trundle at my feet. The brittle leaves skating across our windows sounded too much like hands scratching to get in. I heard every little noise in the sighing house. No scuttle in the walls got past me.

Then one night I knew someone was down in the kitchen. I'd dreamed of Noah and somehow thought he'd found his way home. I'd dreamed his hand was knocking at the kitchen door. Some stirring from below brought me around, and I came bolt awake. The floorboards were cold when I put a careful foot out of bed.

At the top of the stairs I saw no light from the kitchen. Still, somebody was there. I wished for Paw's fowling piece as I started down with nothing in my hands. I was quiet, but anything with ears could hear the popping of the stairs.

The only light came from the last embers on the hearth. A figure stood there by the kitchen table. In the first moment it was a haunt with long, tangled gray hair hiding its face. Hearing me, the ghost turned, and I saw who it was.

"Mama?" I hung there in the doorway.

I hadn't startled her. She seemed to think she'd sent for me, and maybe she had. She stood there in her old night-dress worn paper-thin, without a shawl. "Mama, you'll catch your death."

"I hope I do," she said. "I can't live like this. I want him back."

"Mama, we all want him back."

"He's bad sick, you know," she said. "He is. I know things. Where do you think Cass gets it? She gets it from me. I want him back. Go get him."

She rapped the table with her knuckles. I imagine now her eyes burned brighter than the embers, like something crouching out in the timber. I felt the heat of her eyes on my face.

"Did you hear me?" she said in a terrible whisper. "He's sick. My boy's sick. Go to him. Nurse him till he can travel. Then bring him back to me."

It wasn't Mama at all. The floor yawned at my feet.

"Are you deaf?" she said in a cold voice I'd never heard.

"Mama, if I could find him, they wouldn't let me have him. He's a soldier." My head throbbed. How could I reason with her? "If he got well, Mama, they'd send him into battle."

"Go get him," she said, hearing nothing. "Wait till daylight. Then get out. Don't come back without him."

I was crying like a lost child now. This wasn't the Mama I'd known. Who was this heartless stranger?

"Mama, I can't. I wouldn't know how. You and me'll go. We'll look for Noah together."

She laughed then, and I wish I could forget that laugh. "I see what you'd do. You'd lure me away from this house. And what if he's started home already? What if he come home and found me gone?"

She whipped around, quick, her hair flying, like she heard Noah's footfall on the porch. And I saw I'd lost her. She'd been whittled to madness by her fear.

She looked back at me, one last time. The merciful dark hid her face. "I waited for his paw to come home. I wore out with waiting, and what for? I won't wait for Noah. I ain't got that kind of time now. Don't come back without him. I can spare you. I can't spare him."

That blow sent me staggering. I'd have cut and run from her, but another figure stood behind me in the shadows of the hall, another ghostly figure. I was too numb for fear now. It was Calinda, tall as the door in the long pillar of her nightdress. She was always to be Calinda to me. Her real name, her African name, CoinCoin, came from too far away. I wanted to throw myself into her arms. I needed to be in somebody's arms.

"Light a lamp," Calinda said. She'd heard it all, or enough. With a shaking hand I brought fire on a straw from the last ember to the lamp. Mama had slumped onto a chair. She was staring away from me, as if I should be gone already.

"This one, we take her up to her bed," Calinda said, and we did. We got Mama between us, and she even leaned on me, heavy up the stairs. But when we got her into bed, she turned her face to the wall.

Still, it wasn't daylight. We went back down to the kitchen, and Calinda made a pot of her powerful New Orleans coffee.

It didn't warm me. The cold of the floor climbed my legs. My heart was frozen. I reeled at how quick my life had come to an end. I couldn't go, and I couldn't stay.

I didn't doubt but that Noah was sick. He'd have the trots by now, the way they were eating. We'd heard about the pneumonia the boys had brought with them from the wet ground they'd slept on at Jacksonville. We knew about the measles, and there was typhoid talk. Dr. Hutchings had said Cairo was a pesthole.

But how could I go? I didn't know where the world was, nor how to get there.

Gray light streaked the window. Calinda sat across the

table from me, hung in shawls, warming her long hands on the mug. "Me, I stay at 'ome," she said a moment before I asked her to go with me. "I see to things here."

Calinda was such a miser with her words that you believed every one of them. Still, I had to say, "But they's sickness down there, and you know the cures." Did it dawn on me that I was asking her to help her enemies, if that's what our side was to her?

Her arms were folded now, and her face seemed darker in the brightening day. "I send the cures with you, you and Delphine."

Delphine? What earthly good would—

"If you go among men," Calinda said, "she come in handy. She is meant for men." And Calinda said no more.

We went to Cairo, Delphine and me, in the great journey of my life. We went to try and find Noah, if he was alive, and bring him back if we could. Delphine was fierce to go, though whether it was monotony that moved her or love for Noah, I was in no position to ask.

It took us some days to get ready. Cass and Calinda combed the timber for jimsonweed and bloodwort and all the cures we were to take with us. We emptied out our sick drawer, and gathered up all the lumps of our good homemade soap, and all the eats we could carry: pots of this and jars of that, wrapped in Noah's warm winter clothes, and all the quilts we could force into the trunks. Two trunks too heavy for us to shift on our own, a hamper, and a hatbox.

Delphine needed dress upon dress, her stays and chemises and everything else that went underneath. And cloaks and capes because November was nearly upon us, and a dozen pair of gloves. Her chlorine toothwash. Even her cut-coral necklace. On our last night at home, she retrimmed two traveling hats for us, with close veils.

I supposed we'd wait for the next boat heading south. But Delphine wouldn't hear of it. Who knew when the next boat would stop? Besides, she'd had an unpleasant experience on a boat at Cairo. We'd go on the train. My mind flickered and went blank at the thought. I'd never seen a train nor the tracks it ran on. It meant rounding up Pegleg Snelson and his buckboard to carry us and our boxes over to Carbondale—miles and miles of bad road. It meant going in the middle of the night to get there in time to meet the train. It meant stepping off the Backbone into thin air for me, who'd never been out of the county.

We did a big baking that last afternoon, biscuits that would pack better than loaves. Cass wrung the necks off four big friers she knew by name. Birds flopped headless in the yard, then popped in the pan. We ate hearty ourselves, and Cass put aside all the drumsticks and gizzards, Noah's favorites. I couldn't meet her eye when she handed me the hamper. I dared not promise her Noah. But I see her yet in my mind, holding out her offering.

In all this frenzy, Calinda took the time to lay out her cards and give them a reading. She often did, but this evening when Cass peered over her shoulder to see the cards for herself, Calinda sent her away. She pointed a long finger to the far side of the room, and Cass went.

After Calinda had studied the cards with special care, she scooped them up, and something passed between her and Delphine. Something just that quick, no more than a word or two in one of their languages.

I couldn't have slept. When I was ready to go with my hat on, I stood in the darkness at the door of Mama's room. She lay still as a dead woman in the bed, her head turned away. But the house was astir around her. She was awake. I stood there to let her know I was going because she could spare me.

Chapter Ten

The Illinois Central locomotive made straight for us. At the sight of that one-eyed iron thing, I'd have run off across plowed ground if I wasn't afraid it would follow me. It lumbered into the station at Carbondale and shook the world. Live steam shot at our skirttails, and the sound was deafening.

Delphine was naturally unfazed. While we'd waited in the depot, she'd sent a message by telegraph to Cairo, in hopes it would find Dr. Hutchings for whatever good he might do us. To send word by a wire was well beyond my imaginings.

At the platform the engine seemed to claw the ground like a living thing. Delphine directed our trunks into the baggage car. The train was a long one, crammed with military supplies. We were handed up into the only chair car.

It was nearly full of men stirring from their sleep for a look at Delphine behind her veils. Two of them give up their seats for us. With a sickening lurch we pulled out of the station and gathered speed. I'd kept the hamper with me in case we were hungry on the train, but I left my stomach at Carbondale.

I'd never moved this fast. It was like a dream of flying. The hills and hollers of Southern Illinois blurred past the window, red and yellow under the autumn sun. I learned now a purpose for the veils Delphine had tacked to our hats. Soot and ash blew continually through the open window.

My veil plastered against my nose with every breath I drew. Delphine's veil, with dots that gave her beauty marks, hung in a graceful swag, caught up by a corsage of cloth flowers on her shoulder.

She could have been any age behind her veils, beneath the dip of her hat brim. I sat opposite her, yearning for one crumb of her confidence because I needed it now. The two men in officer's uniforms sitting beside us got up to smoke their cheroots at the end of the car. I asked her then what I'd never managed to ask before.

"Delphine, how old are you?"

"Me?" Her eyebrows flew up behind the spotted veil. I wondered if she'd tell me, but she shrugged and said, "Fifteen."

I nearly fainted and fell back in sheer surprise.

"Sixteen at Christmas. Calinda, she is seventeen."

"Never! Why, you're younger than me!" Only months, but I'd been looking up to her all this time.

She shrugged again. "For me, it is not young." She withdrew a gloved hand from her muff and pointed to herself. "Much should have been decided for me by now, my future made certain."

"You don't mean married?"

"Married?" She turned the word over like it was a new one to her. Then she jammed both fists back into her muff where she hid the money for our journey.

"We don't marry," she said. "Not as you know it."

The men came back to their seats, and she looked away out the window to discourage them if they tried to speak to us. I did the same, wondering what I'd heard her say, wondering if I'd heard her right.

We smelled Cairo before we saw the place. It was the end of the line. In better times this train ran all the way to New Orleans to connect with the ships to Panama. All the mob milling on the platform outside looked like tough customers. I was too scared to stir. But Delphine turned to the two officers beside us.

"You will be good enough to help us with our trunks?" she said, like it was the least they could do. They fell over themselves to hand her down onto the platform, and me too since I wouldn't turn loose of her.

I was occupied then in keeping my skirts off the filthy platform. It was littered with busted boxes and crates broken open with their labels gone. Food of every kind rotted on the ground: broken crocks of fruit and splintered jars of jam, cured hams crusted with flies, loaves of bread frosted with mold. It was the provisions families had tried to send their soldier sons, poorly packed and too long in the journey. The combination of smells cut my eyes. But worse smells were on the way.

The crowds parted, and there like a knight in armor was Dr. Hutchings, lifting his hat to us. He'd found our message when he'd come to the telegraph office to wire for supplies. And yes, there was a place where we could stay, though the town was bursting at the seams and they wanted two prices for everything.

Oh, it was good to see him, though he looked tired to death. He'd slept in them clothes. Still, he seemed younger than I'd remembered. He had a trap pulled by a piebald pony, tied up by the platform. The officers swung our trunks up onto the back of the trap and melted away once they saw a gentleman had met us.

I made sure Delphine was up on the board beside the doctor, to reward him for coming to find us. When I'd hunkered among the boxes behind, we set off through streets deep in mud and worse.

Cairo crouched in a swamp under the levees that held back both rivers, the Ohio and the Mississippi. I couldn't have pictured a town this big. The endless rows of houses, one right after the other, crowded me. Long trains of army wagons drawn by mules clogged the streets and slowed our way.

The filth of the place was beyond anything you ever seen. Along all the mud streets water stood in the ditches, abuzz with bluebottles and mosquitoes, as there hadn't been a frost yet this far south. The whole town was a dump. The swollen carcasses of dogs lay about, and even a dead horse half in a cut of water red with its blood. I clutched the hamper to me and tried to cover my nose. It was a terrible place, this Cairo, right down there at the end of Illinois, at the end of the world.

People swarmed wherever you looked. Men mainly, of every age. Most were in uniform or parts of uniform. Some went about their business, but more of them were drunk—reeling drunk and fighting drunk and sleeping it off with their boots in the ditches and their heads cradled in filth.

"They train on the parade grounds all morning," the doctor said, "but nobody can decide what to do with them the rest of the day. The able-bodied."

The ruts turned us into another street where the houses were bigger. Dr. Hutchings drove up the lane of quite a fine place, finer than any in Grand Tower. He had a room here from a widow woman, a Mrs. Hanrahan. "She's a Southern lady," he said, "indeed, a Southern sympathizer, I gather." This may have been for Delphine's benefit. She'd seen nothing welcoming in this town so far.

Dr. Hutchings said Mrs. Hanrahan had a full house, but

there was a summer kitchen around back where we could sleep. She'd have her handyman set up beds for us out there by nightfall.

But what did I care where I slept? I was here to find my brother. I plagued Dr. Hutchings about him before he'd seen me down from the trap. He pulled on his beard when he told me about Noah. Yes, he was in one of the Thirty-first regimental hospitals. "He's over the worst," the doctor said, "with any luck."

And it wasn't measles. It was dysentery, according to the doctor who was too refined and scientific to say trots.

The summer kitchen was a little black-shuttered one-room shanty overgrown with brilliant sumac. An iron range stood inside, the first kitchen stove I ever set eyes on.

When we threw open the trunks, the doctor brightened at the sight of Calinda's cures, the horehound and lobelia and the jimsonweed painkiller. They seemed to be short of everything here. We folded what we could carry in a quilt, and I was ready to set off.

But Dr. Hutchings thought we ought to pin up our skirts because the campgrounds were a quagmire. He was a little shy of the female sex, for he looked away when he spoke of our skirts and the heels on Delphine's slippers. He stood out on the porch, examining the sumac, while we made these adjustments.

What a sight I'd have been. My brown-striped calico was hitched up to show my broken boots. But I wore my hat and veils, elegant because Delphine had seen to them.

There was a full bird on the wing, stuffed, about to take off from my hat brim. I know there was because of the picture we had taken later.

Delphine seemed to think I ought to drop to my knees and lace up her flat-heeled boots. I wouldn't because once you started waiting on her, there was no end to it. I came this close to telling her I wasn't her slave, but thought better of it. Batting at her veils, she managed to bend over and lace up her own boots with much sighing and grunting on account of her corsets.

Then we were ready with some afternoon left. Off we went through the terrible Cairo streets, making for Noah.

They'd pitched Camp Defiance out on the point where the Ohio River runs into the muddy Mississippi. The great earthworks that held back the rivers were the fortress walls. Cannons bristled on top. Some were trained across at Kentucky, some across at Missouri, rebel country both ways.

The front gate was only an opening in a rail stockade fence. The families of soldiers crowded around outside, waiting for them. But Dr. Hutchings had passes into the camp for us, though we were to be off the post before they fired the sunset gun.

It was a tent city inside, row on row of white tents, close as teeth. The first ones were raised over wooden floors. These were where the officers were quartered. And will I ever forget the first real sight there was to see?

A great cart wheel, six feet across, leaned against a

flagpole. Tied hand and foot to that wheel, spread-eagle, was a soldier boy—no older than Noah. He was burned by the sun, and his tongue lolled out of his mouth. Around his neck a sign hung on twine:

THIEF

He wasn't Noah, but he was somebody's son. I saw then I was going to have to be stronger than I was.

"Military justice is rough justice," Dr. Hutchings said, "or no justice at all." But he went on to say he'd end up in uniform, doctoring for the army. He had thought he'd do more good as a "contract surgeon," a civilian doctor, but he was finding out different.

The camp roads were worse than Cairo's. We were up to our hubs now. These were meaner tents back here, for the regular soldiers, pitched right in the mud against the seeping levee. The reek of cooking fires hung low over worse smells. We were pretty nearly mired now. Dr. Hutchings helped Delphine and me down on the only dry patch. He said he'd go see if Noah was up to coming out to us.

"But where is he?" Delphine demanded to know, gazing about for anything resembling a hospital.

"There are six regimental hospitals," Dr. Hutchings said. "Those three tents are one of them."

"We go there." Delphine hiked her shortened skirts.

"Oh no, Miss Duval." The doctor put out a hand to bar her way—never a good idea. "They're under quarantine.

Most of them are measles cases. Half the regiment has had—"

"Me, I am a Creole from New Orleans." Delphine struck herself a blow. "If yellow fever can't kill me, what can? And what does this girl care for measles?" She indicated me. "She want her brother."

"But no women—ladies—are allowed in the hospital tents. It's entirely for your own good. The men are in their underwear, and there are no blankets and . . ." Dr. Hutchings was getting right down to the end of his rope.

Delphine had drawn up to her almost five feet without the heeled slippers. She glanced back at me, and her veiled eyes sparked their dark fire. "This girl's brother is in that tent. Is it so?"

Dr. Hutchings admitted it was.

"You are not an officer to command me. And me, I am not a soldier." She pointed herself out with a gloved finger. "And if I was, I wouldn't be soldiering on this side. Get the quilt," she said to me.

The doctor was this close to wringing his hands. "Truly, Miss Pruitt," he said as we bore down on the tent flap, "I can't permit—" But it would have taken five or six men his size to keep us out. I wanted my brother.

Delphine, with the hamper on her arm, ducked inside and stopped dead. I walked up her heels, with the quilt bundled in both hands. The smell hit me, and nearly sent me sideways. Delphine swayed like a sapling. The doctor edged in beside, with some last-ditch notion of sparing us the worst.

I supposed it was a tent for four or five. There were ten in there, five on a side. In the middle a Sibley stove smoked and used up what air there was. Two or three boys were on cots. The rest were stretched right out on the ground in beds of stinking straw.

They lay there where they'd been sick. They sprawled in their messes because they were too weak to get to the privies, if there were privies. In the afternoon light slanting through canvas, they looked like old men. One sat at the end of his cot with a bucket and a dipper at his feet. He was badly wasted, and his cheeks were sunk to where he looked like a death's-head. "Tilly?" he said.

Noah. It was Noah. We couldn't faint nor flee now. We threw back our veils and made our way to him, sinking in the slime with every step. None of the prone figures marked our passage, though some were wide-eyed.

"Delphine?"

I wouldn't have known him in the street. But they were Noah's eyes, blue and keen. I saw he'd already decided to live, though he needed encouragement.

He pointed at the bundle I'd made of the quilt. His fingers were long and gaunt now. "You pieced that quilt, Tilly." And so I had, in my coarse stitches, using thread of whatever color I could find. The tears flooded his eyes and swam down all the hollows of his face. A boy's tears for home and what had been.

He tried to hide them from Delphine, but it didn't matter. Her temper flared up like sudden sunrise, and she sputtered into French: "*Mon Dieu, c'est incroyable!* It is—how do you call this place? A sty. Who nurses these men?"

"I'm the nurse," Noah said. "Them that can get up off their pallets is the nurses. It's the army way. We can't get any other help in here for fear they'll catch the measles. I ought to have brung the boys water, but I ain't worked up the steam." He touched the empty pail with the toe of his boot. He wore his boots from home.

Dr. Hutchings hovered. Delphine was just about to hold him personally responsible for the entire war on all fronts. I grabbed up the pail and handed it over. I didn't know if a doctor would lower himself to tote water, but this one was glad enough to make himself scarce. Delphine and me both knew he had a good heart, and he was stretched thin. But he was a man, and men can't look after themselves, let alone one another.

"Could you eat something?" I asked Noah. I longed to take a cake of pine tar soap to his neck and ears, but first things first.

"I could eat real good," he said, "if I could get it and it was cooked through." We showed him the hamper. "Fried chicken?" he said in a thick and wondering voice.

"They was strutting around Cass's chicken yard this time yesterday, eatin' bugs," I told him, and watched him light into a leg. He was starved. The dysentery had wrung him out, but he was past that now and weak mostly from hunger. We had the biscuits too, and I fished a jar of preserves out of the quilt.

Delphine and me, we stood over him while he wept at the chicken and then gnawed it to white bone. Then he sobbed at the sight of the biscuit and put it away, both halves heaped with preserves. Oh, it done me good to see him feed.

But wedged beside him on the filthy cot I spied a book he'd been studying. It was Hardee's *Tactics,* a text about soldiering and great battles and how they were waged. My heart sank. Noah was too weak to heft a bucket of water, and still he was studying the arts of war, and yearning to let fly with grape and canister.

I marveled at the way men's minds are made and how they think, if you can call it thought at all. I saw plain that we'd get him on his feet only so he could go off and try his level best to get himself killed. I could have wept, but I thought I better save my tears for when I'd need them most.

Chapter Eleven

We made a bare beginning that first afternoon. The doctor watered the boys, and said that the measles cases could handle fried chicken. They were easy to locate because of the scabs.

I'll say this for Delphine. Once she turned back her sleeves, she went to work. She'd never worked that hard before, and I can witness that she never worked that hard again. But when she set her mind to something, or lapsed into French, you just as well get out of her road.

She left Noah to me, and I wondered if it was modesty. I had to get him out of the underwear he had on. That suit of underwear could just about stand up by itself. Delphine gave Noah a wide berth and ministered to the others.

When we had to leave, I turned away to give her a moment with him, if she wanted it. He wasn't clean enough to kiss, not to mention the witnesses. But she didn't tarry, so I couldn't tell if she loved my brother or not. She drew down her veils, and we slogged out of the tent. I'd have thrown my boots away if I'd had another pair.

On our way back to the summer kitchen, I wouldn't have minded riding up beside Dr. Hutchings, for the pleasure of his company. But I made sure Delphine rode up there by him instead. He needed a little starch in his spine, and she was the one to put it there. Sure enough, she lectured him at length about the passes we'd need every day now. There was a nip in the evening air, so she spoke out about blankets for the boys. We didn't have quilts enough for all.

When the doctor said he lacked the authority to "requisition" blankets, Delphine told him to find the authority double quick and she didn't want to have to mention it again. She'd been shook by what she'd seen of an army hospital, and instead of calling for her smelling salts, she got her dander up.

I was just behind them in the trap, taking in every word. Seemed to me that when it came time to marry, Dr. Hutchings would need a wife with a lighter touch than Delphine's. He looked pretty well whipsawed when he lifted us down at the back of Mrs. Hanrahan's place.

We lived in her summer kitchen throughout our time in Cairo. The widow Hanrahan wanted seven dollars a week from us, and she wanted it up front. She sent her handyman down to collect our rent that first evening. Seven dollars! There were houses all over Grand Tower you could buy outright for seven dollars, and they'd throw in the fencing and dig you a well. But then, Mrs. Hanrahan was a rich woman, and the rich didn't get that way by giving you a bargain.

As we kept being told, we were lucky to have a roof over us. I for one had never lived in such luxury, as the summer kitchen had all the city conveniences. The pump was just to one side of the porch, and the privy just to the rear. The big iron stove inside heated water for our laundry and washing ourselves. It took the chill off the evenings, and I was to fry up a deal of chicken through many a night, once we got Dr. Hutchings to requisition the chickens and the stovewood.

The beds were draped with mosquito bars, and were comfortable enough if you were as tired every night as we were. And beneath them, a chamber pot apiece—china ones.

I was more dead than alive when we got back that first night. But Delphine had to unpack all her dresses, shake them out, and hang them around the room. She had brought her gold hand mirror with the violets on the back. And the portrait of her papa in its gilt frame, the yellow-haired

Monsieur Jules Duval. She hung him above her cot, for she went nowhere without him.

Mrs. Hanrahan didn't see fit to pay us a call in our early days there. She was a busy woman, according to Dr. Hutchings. Rich Cairo people in big houses took in sick officers to nurse them. So in addition to Dr. Hutchings, she had three or four ailing officers in her spare rooms. One of them was from U. S. Grant's personal staff. These invalids lolled in starched sheets, seen to by servants, while the regular soldiers slept on the cold ground in their filth. But then if there was justice in this world, you wouldn't look for it in Cairo.

And if you ask me, some of them officers were none too poorly. They sat out on the gallery of an evening, smoking their El Sol seegars and drinking from small silver cups, and I doubt if it was medicine.

Our days at Camp Defiance overlap in my mind. But each day Noah was stronger—tottering, then helping out, then growing restless. We wanted to get them all on their feet, at least well enough to carry their own slops and feed themselves.

We only lost one, a boy from up around Belleville. And he was too far gone when we got there. He starved to death because he couldn't keep anything down. Delphine spoiled two of her dresses, trying to feed him. You wouldn't have known her. When he died in her arms, she closed his eyes, folded his hands on his poor shrunken chest, and looked away with her mouth pulled into a straight line. I can't tell you more about it. I can't bear to bring it back.

Seeing her lovely face floating over them may have pulled several through, but you couldn't call her an angel of mercy. When some of the boys lacked the spirit to eat or stir themselves, she was apt to say, "You will need all your strength when you come against the Confederates! They are a real army! They rarely sicken and never retreat!" So I suppose her greatest achievement was that she wasn't shot as a traitor.

As they improved, they wanted to know our names, especially hers. But I was popular too because I was Noah Pruitt's sister. His Company C was made up mostly of Jackson County boys, and they told us of home, of sisters and sweethearts, and the tears flowed.

We got our boys well enough and fed to where they could shovel out the tent down to dry ground. That was after we found out where the army hid its shovels. We made a bonfire of the straw they'd slept on, once we found fresh straw. I boiled their long-handled underwear over an open fire, and that underwear teemed and swarmed with living things that glistened and crawled. I itch to think of it now.

No able-bodied loafer outside our tent was safe from us. We had jobs for each and all, sending them for kindling and straw and whatever they could find. We put them to work, and anybody not skinning could hold a leg, as the saying went.

We got some loafer to find us a bunch of them big nail

kegs. You could saw them in two and caulk them. Then the boys could take baths in them. Of course they wouldn't strip nekkid until the sunset gun had seen Delphine and me off the post.

We got our boys clean and stretched out on fresh, sweet straw. We dosed them with our cures and cooked their rations for them. We made a believer out of Dr. Hutchings, and no army doctor come around to put a stop to us. We sang some too because the boys liked it.

Delphine could offer up a rendition of "My Old Kentucky Home," flavored in her French, that brought a lump to many a Yankee throat, including mine. And we sang a song the whole country was singing that fall of 1861, though I thought it must have been written expressly for me.

Brother, tell me of the battle,
How the soldiers fought and fell,
Tell me of the weary marches,
She who loves will listen well.

Brother, draw thee close beside me,
Lay your head upon my breast
While you're telling of the battle,
Let your fevered forehead rest.

We slept fast and deep through the brief nights, and hardly had the time to look up from our days, or to notice that we weren't girls anymore.

All around us the camp girded for war on the river. Black Jack Logan, who commanded the Thirty-first, spoke of hewing their way to the Gulf with their swords. Colonel White come to our tent to see who was fit enough to train, and took Noah away.

Back he hobbled in a pair of stiff new boots, carrying an ancient Belgian musket he said hadn't been fired since Napoleon's day. The sabers rattled around us.

The Confederate general, Leonidas Polk, held the Mississippi not twenty miles south of Cairo. His rebs were dug in on both sides of the river, at Columbus, Kentucky, and at the steamboat landing of Belmont, Missouri. U. S. Grant was expected to move downriver and "make a demonstration" against the reb positions any minute now.

Then one day they issued Noah his full uniform. It was so shoddy that Delphine said it would melt in the first rain. And it was so big on him he looked like a little ear of corn in too many husks. But he was ready to fight now, and I braced myself for the attack.

It come quicker than I thought, quicker than a striking snake when you least looked for it. And that attack come not at the camp nor on the river. It come to the summer kitchen.

Chapter Twelve

We'd been her tenants better than a week before Mrs. Hanrahan come down her garden path to see how we were doing.

We'd settled in by then, Delphine and me. It was just evening, and we'd turned up the lamp. We had mending to do for the boys. The widow provided us wicks, but charged us extra for the lamp oil.

We heard her before we seen her, coming along the path. It seemed she was with Dr. Hutchings. "Ah declare, Doctor," sang out a Southern accent thick enough to plant cotton in, "Ah been remiss in my duties to them young ladies. But then nobody knows better than yourself how worked Ah am."

Delphine settled her skirts, took up her needle, and made quite a pretty picture of herself there by lamplight when I opened the door.

On the porch Mrs. Hanrahan clung to Dr. Hutchings's arm in an unseemly way, or so I thought. She was twice his age and gaunt under her shawls. But sharp-eyed.

She'd have breezed straight in, but the doctor detained her on the threshold to introduce me. "May I present Miss Tilly Pruitt of Grand Tower," he said in that formal way he had.

"Ah declare, ain't you pretty, honey," she said, looking past me. She wore a noisy silk dress. A big cross of ebonized wood swung from a chain around her neck.

Delphine glanced up from her work in the glowing room. Mrs. Hanrahan's hard gaze fell on her and jarred something inside me. Her eyes scanned the place—the hanging dresses, the portrait of Delphine's papa. Then she was looking at Delphine again.

Drawing away from Dr. Hutchings, she propped a fist on her hip and said, "Well, well, what have we here?"

Another silence fell while the doctor saw he was in a room with too many women. She turned to him, showing us her hawk's profile. "Ah declare, Doctor, just see what you have brought me. A colored gal."

What had she said? I reached out for something to hold on to.

Delphine put her mending aside. She didn't rise. She

settled back and sighed, as if this had been a long time coming.

"I am of the *gens de couleur, madame,*" she said, calmly proud. "The free people of color, if you speak no French."

"I know what you are," our landlady snapped. "I've lived down in New Orleans."

"You have been in New Orleans, *madame,*" Delphine said, "but you are not of it. Irish, are you, from the name?"

"And no quadroon wench is going to talk me down like shanty Irish. I know New Orleans better than what you think. Enough to wonder what a picture strongly resemblin' Jules Duval is doin' on the wall of my summer kitchen."

"He is my *papa.*" Delphine struggled with herself now, holding on to the chair arms.

Mrs. Hanrahan grinned, like Delphine had given herself away. "I thought so. Big planter, ain't he, with holdin's up along the False River? And a white family up there?"

Delphine looked away from the light.

"And you're one of his colored family, ain't you? Seems like I seen your mother, very high and mighty, in her carriage on Royal Street."

"She would hardly go on foot," Delphine remarked.

"And she's sent you up here, ain't she? Because if the South loses the war, you'll be nothin' better than a freed slave. You're not much higher in the world than that right now. If the Yankees take New Orleans, that fancy life of yours'll come crashin' down. You'll be no better than them they sell on the auction block. Up here you're light enough to pass. But, gal, you don't fool me. I'm no Yankee. I ain't that dumb."

Another silence. Dr. Hutchings stood like a figure carved in stone.

"Do you want me off your place?" Delphine said without a trace of accent. And ready to go.

"Lands, no," Mrs. Hanrahan said. "I want your rent money. And you're in an outbuilding at the back of my property where you belong. Doctor, if you'll be good enough to see me back to the house."

She waited, then turned to him, her eyes narrowing.

"I think I won't, Mrs. Hanrahan," he said.

We waited until she banged the door to behind her.

I was as near to Delphine as I am to you, but I didn't want to put out my hand if she didn't want to take it. All I could think of was what a terrible place the world is. What a mean, ugly, hard place. I swore if I ever got back to Grand Tower, they'd have to bind and gag me and drag me behind a mule to get me out of town again.

The quiet went on and on until Delphine said, "They hate us, you know. The Irish. They come hungry and work cheap. The yellow fever lays them low. And we were there before them. Our roots are in New Orleans mud. We people of color make the city work. It is like no other place because of us. We were there from the earliest times. They despise us for our ease, for our silken lives. They don't understand how people of color can be free." She looked away from us. "Almost free."

That explained something, though very little. I drew the doctor into the circle of light. Without thinking about it, I took his hand and pulled him nearer. And now I reached for Delphine and took them both in hand.

"Delphine, tell us who you are," I said, hoping she'd trust us enough. But she was Delphine, so she had to spin a romance tale out of it, or try her best to.

"My *grandmère,* she was one of *Les Sirènes.* Legends are told of these beauties who flee the slaves' uprising on the island of *Saint-Domingue,* years and years ago. She is carried by her *maman* to Cuba, then *Nouvelle Orléans.* And ev'ry white man is at her feet. She choose one and my *maman* is born, lovelier still.

"My *maman,* she choose Monsieur Jules Duval, and I am born."

She opened her hands, presenting herself. I blundered into this silence. "But you said, 'We never marry.' You said that on the train."

The doctor made a move to still me.

"We cannot marry white men," she said, patient with my Yankee ignorance. "The Spanish make a law against such marriage. The French make a law. There is a law now. But New Orleans prefer its customs to the law. Our white fathers buy our mothers fine homes in all the best streets, in Chartres Street. And if there is a daughter, she is brought up by her mother to find a future with a white gentleman of her own. A man of substance. We have a name for this. It is *plaçage.* A respectable arrangement."

She looked at me then, her worldliest look yet. "If this

war did not threaten ev'rything, I would have my own home now. My own protector. Perhaps . . ." She looked down at herself and fell silent.

It was a gate swung open on yet another world I didn't know. Was there no end to what I didn't know?

"That woman called you a name," I said.

"Quadroon? Our society is often called that. There are the quadroon balls, you know, each Wednesday night at the Salle d'Orleans where gentlemen—white gentlemen—come to pay us court.

"Quadroon, octoroon. There are these names." She shrugged grandly. "I am a *femme de couleur libre,* a free woman of color. French blood flow through me and Spanish blood and African blood. It is the African blood they despise. Is it not curious?"

She saw me gazing at her arm resting there on the table in the lamplight. I'd always thought her skin was the color of a peach, warmed by the Southern sun.

She drew back her sleeve. "I am nearly as white as you, *chère.* There are others like me paler than yourself, blue-eyed, yellow-haired. Yet as our saying goes, there is a tignon in the family."

My head whirled, at all this, and her bravery.

"If all is lost for us, I go find another life. *Maman,* she would give me up to give me my chance. I am her treasure." Tears beaded her lavish lashes. "If it is my fate, I go among those who know nothing, who cannot speak to me as that woman does tonight."

"You were going to St. Louis," I said, "when—"

"Mais non, chère." She shook her head, weary. "I have no aunt. We know no one beyond our world. We free people of color live on a kind of island, lapped by a sea of slavery. Beyond that sea is this territory up here." She gazed around the room. "Like the mountains of the moon to us.

"We would have gone ashore at Cairo because we hear the North begin here. But we take fright when the boat is boarded."

"And they robbed you of your pearl-handled pistol," I said.

"Yes, they do that. We dare not come ashore, even before we know what kind of place this Cairo is."

"And so—"

"Your Grand Tower is the next stop of the boat. It is, perhaps, fate?"

And that was something else I didn't know.

I felt my way along now, word by word, though it was too late to be careful. "Delphine, seems like your people need a lot of help, the way you live."

She nodded absently.

"Do your people own slaves?"

"It happens."

"Is Calinda your slave?"

The great fringed violet eyes turned on me. "Ah *ma chère,* she is my sister."

Chapter Thirteen

On the day Noah sailed away to fight the rebs for the river, we somehow got him to the photographer's shop. The picture stands on the table by my bed.

I remember the stench of the chemicals in the photographer's shop, though it smelled no worse than the rest of Cairo. We had to stand stock-still for an eternity to get the picture made. Then the glass plate with our image slipped out of the photographer's hand and exploded on the floor. Delphine took that as a bad omen, and of course we had it all to do over again.

There we are, trapped in time, Delphine and me on either side of Noah. I stare straight ahead from under the bird on my hat like I'm resigned to being shot at sunrise. I'd thrown back my veils, but Delphine didn't. She looks through them, forever a woman of mystery, and not quite sixteen. Her hands hide in the muff where the last of our money was living. She wears her cut-coral necklace and two or three of her best paisley shawls. She's dressed to kill, as the saying went, though Noah really is.

He stands between us in his forage cap, proud in his big new uniform that he seems to be peering out of, not wearing. But his arms hang stiff at his sides, the cuffs to his knuckles, a soldier boy before the battle. There's something missing in his eyes, a vacancy, as if he couldn't wait and has gone on ahead.

In all the turmoil of that last day, we didn't find Dr. Hutchings in time, though it would have made a better picture with him in it. Then not half an hour later we met him in the street. Even as he touched the bill of his cap, I had to look twice to know him. He was in uniform now, with a captain's bars on his shoulders. He'd joined up in time to sail with Grant's forces.

It was November 6, and the command came through to cook a day's rations and prepare to embark. In the end, Colonel Logan could muster only a little over six hundred infantry, as so many boys were still down sick. But Noah was fit to fight. I'd seen to that.

The Thirty-first joined the other regiments marching under U. S. Grant, three thousand strong. They sailed that evening in a chill mist, and Delphine and I stood in the throng down by the wharves to see them off. Dr. Hutchings had urged us to go home to Grand Tower, to put Cairo and Mrs. Hanrahan behind us.

But I couldn't go empty-handed, without Noah. It wasn't me Mama wanted.

The streets were already a churn of red mud when the three thousand tramped past us, some of them staggering drunk, and singing as they came:

The Rebs have taken the best of me legs,
Bad luck to the chap that hit it,
If Uncle Sam gives me a cork for me stump,
I hope 'twill be one that will fit it.

We searched those marchers, rank and file, for Noah. But he blended with all that blue, vanished already. Did I look for Dr. Hutchings? I don't remember now.

They set sail on four great transport ships. Noah's Thirty-first marched aboard the *Alex Scott.* Two wooden gunboats, the *Tyler* and the *Lexington,* followed after. That wide stretch where the two big rivers boil together was crowded with turning boats. We watched them away in the night, hearing voices over the water singing "Yankee Doodle."

We stood in the crowd of mothers and fathers, sisters and sweethearts, falling silent as the boats disappeared around that bend down by Wickliffe, Kentucky. The street lighting in Cairo was just about what you'd expect, but some of the men had fired torches to see the boys aboard the boats.

I looked at Delphine. The flames were dim, and she'd always been darker than I'd noticed. But in the flicker of torchlight, I read her face and saw her soul. She loved my brother. And she was mourning him already.

"Delphine, did you tell him who you are?"

"Perhaps I don't have to," she said, in a despairing voice.

Now I knew why she hadn't lifted a finger to nurse him in the hospital tent, why she was always turning away from him to the others. She'd hoped he'd be too sick to die.

It was famous, the Battle of Belmont, Missouri. It sparked the career of General U. S. Grant and led him in time to the White House as President. It was the first struggle for the Mississippi, that great highway flowing between my Grand Tower and Delphine's New Orleans. As in many a battle before it and since, both sides claimed victory. But no woman would have called it a victory.

People stood on the levees all day, hearing the thunder of the guns rolling up the river valley. In the afternoon, smoke drifted on the horizon as if a sizable place had been put to the torch.

On the next morning Delphine and me were on the wharf before daybreak, wound in our shawls against the damp morning as we watched for the returning boats. There came a flash of light as the first of them rounded the bend, then the others behind it. We heard music wavering over the water. It was a steam calliope, so one of the warships had once been a showboat. It was playing a funeral dirge,

"O Rest in the Lord." The sound of a showboat calliope sending this grieving music on ahead hung ever after in my mind.

We pushed forward in the mob when the first gangplank came down. The able-bodied carried the wounded on litters. Now we saw sights we'd been spared in the hospital tent. Blood soaked through the stretchers from the stumps of legs until the gangplank ran with it. We heard the cries of the torn and saw a boy who'd been shot full in the face. But it wasn't Noah because this boy's matted hair was black.

No one had witnessed the fruits of war till now. Men in the crowd wept like children. Women shrieked and keened and fell on their knees. But we didn't. We might miss Noah.

What would we have thought if we'd known then how many of the wounded had been left behind on sandbars? I didn't dream they'd leave a dying soldier behind, so I didn't add that to my fears.

The sun stood high in the sky when Dr. Hutchings came down out of a boat. He saw us, and we fought our way through the surge of people. He and I were thrust together, and before I could speak, he gripped my hands and said, "I've brought him back, Tilly. But you'll have to work to keep him." Tears stood in his eyes, and I saw he was tired to the point of falling down.

Behind him on a litter borne by two ragged, dirty soldiers was Noah. His face was scraped and powder-burned, and he was a mass of stained bandages. The boys on stretchers went into a big warehouse there by the wharf, and we followed. They laid Noah on the floor in a growing row of the wounded. His eyes were open, but he didn't know Delphine or me. A strong smell came off him.

It was rum. "I had to get him drunk to take his arm," the doctor said. "It was nearly off." Then I saw Noah's left arm was gone. It was only a blunt wad of blood-soaked bandages, no longer than his elbow.

We hung over the feverish boy, and all I could think was that now he won't die in a field somewhere. If he dies now, he dies in our arms.

They were dying all around him, up and down the rows on the warehouse floor. And others had lost their limbs.

"Where is it?" I asked Dr. Hutchings. "I want it."

He looked blank.

"His arm. I want to take it home and bury it. I don't want it to end up in a heap of . . ."

"We were on the boat when I took it," he said. "I put it overboard. I gave it to the river."

And I was satisfied with that. I had to be. And he'd been gentle in his telling. "I gave them all to the river," he said.

They brought back three hundred wounded from the Battle of Belmont. There wasn't a place for Noah in the regimental hospitals. The army had no room for a soldier who couldn't be made whole to fight again. They let us have him.

We nursed him, Delphine and me, in the summer kitchen. Mrs. Hanrahan never come near us, but she had to hear Noah screaming through the night in pain from the arm he didn't have.

We made a pallet on the floor, for he thrashed so, he'd have pitched out of bed. He was still on the battleground in his mind. We bathed him night and day in cold water straight from the pump to fight the fever, and still he didn't know us.

The doctor come in the evenings, dead tired from treating the others, half-asleep in the trap, letting the pony find us. He dressed Noah's stump and saw that the flap of skin that covered it was holding.

We couldn't get any food down him, but Doctor Hutchings devised a kind of milk punch laced with brandy that seemed to nourish him, and quiet him.

We sent no word home. I dared not tell them that we had Noah before I could promise him alive.

"Besides," Delphine said, "Calinda, she would not believe such a letter."

"Why ever not, if I wrote it?"

"To her, Noah is dead. She read it in the cards."

"Then she read them wrong," I said, clenching my chin like a fist.

"She read death in the cards," Delphine said as if I hadn't spoken. "She see the coffin come up the river."

Chapter Fourteen

As Noah grew less fitful, Delphine and I spoke more. We sat in the evenings with our work and talked across the sleeping boy. I couldn't keep from asking her about her papa.

"Delphine, is it true? Does he have another whole family—a white family?"

"But of course," she said. "He has three strapping sons, golden-hair like himself. And two daughters who—how do you say it? Simper."

"Do you know them?"

"*Mais non, chère.* To them I do not exist. But they sit below us at the opera. They are in the first loge. We are in the second."

She'd already made me see her *maman* in my mind's eye. Now I saw how much brighter the diamonds blazed on her mother's darker throat. I saw these two families, their faces lit from the brilliant stage of the opera house that I supposed was like a great showboat gone aground.

Questions bubbled up in me. "Your mama has brought you up to be like herself," I said, "to find a white man to . . . protect you. But what about Calinda?"

Delphine's eyebrows rose in that way they had.

"Does your mama want Calinda to find a white man too?"

Delphine shrugged off that entire notion. "*Mais non.* Our *maman* see early that Calinda has the gift of prophecy and is born with ancient secrets. *Maman* see that Calinda can make her own way in the world."

Still, one question just led to another. "But what if you and Calinda had been boys? Sons instead of daughters?"

Her eyes grew huge. She was forever astonished that I didn't know something she'd never told me. "But we have a brother. Andre. He is sent to Paris, of course. *Papa* sent him to perfect his French, to be educated."

"What will he do when he comes back home?"

"Andre? He never will. He become a Frenchman where people do not ask questions."

I tried to see him in my mind, this sudden brother.

"But not all your young men go off to Paris, do they? Isn't there one you could marry? Really marry?"

Delphine looked away, uninterested. "Perhaps. But it is not what my *maman* want for me."

"But—"

"Ah, *chère,* it does not matter now. We are doom the day the Yankees take New Orleans. It was always, how to say it? A delicate balance."

"But if the South wins—"

She put up a thimbled hand to still me. "It will not. We lose the war. This year. Another year. I dream. I pretend, but it is in the cards. Calinda see it. Why deceive oneself? Her cards are never wrong."

We spoke of Calinda, of course.

"When you first come, we thought Calinda was your slave, your servant anyhow. We reckoned you made her sleep on the floor."

"Pffft," said Delphine. "But we are sisters. We are born in the same bed. We sleep in the same bed. And she take up her full share of it too!"

But no, I misremember. She said that later, after the war. After Calinda had gone from our lives.

Into one of our murmuring, meandering conversations, Noah awoke one evening. He blinked up at us, and knew us. He knew too his arm was gone. I don't know how because he could feel it right to the fingertips for years after. We swept down on him, our skirts collapsing on the floor. There came a moment of perfect happiness then, however much it had cost.

We hung there, waiting for his first words.

“I could eat something,” he said in a croaking voice, “if I could get it and it was cooked through.”

I laughed for pure joy until I wanted to cry. But when I looked deeper into Noah’s eyes, I seen the boy was gone, and so the perfect moment passed.

As quick as Dr. Hutchings said we could, we took Noah home. We packed our traps to leave Cairo forever. On the day we went, Mrs. Hanrahan sent down her handyman to take the crockery out of the summer kitchen and break every piece over the pump outside because Delphine had eaten and drunk from it.

We left that place. Lot’s wife may have looked back, but we didn’t. We had Noah strong enough to travel, and that’s what mattered. I changed the dressing on his arm, then—would you credit it?—he wanted to wear his uniform, bloodstained and mudstained, with the arm pinned up over emptiness.

Dr. Hutchings seen us off at the Cairo depot. When we parted, my hand lingered in his, just long enough to know it was where my hand belonged. But I saw no more of him for all the years until the war was over. He was good to write, from wherever they sent him. I kept the letters and read them over and over until I found myself marking time until their author come back to me.

We traveled in a chair car full of others like Noah, one-armed boys and one-legged boys who’d carved their own crutches. These were the ones who could afford the train fare home. The others struggled and straggled along the sliding gravel of the railroad right-of-way outside the window.

After I settled Delphine and Noah together, I perched across from them with the hamper and her hatbox. We were going home now, and the locomotive wasn't pulling us fast enough to suit me.

Once, Noah reached across himself to touch Delphine's hand and said, "I won't be helpless."

I held my breath for her answer. So much seemed to depend on it. Then she turned those vast violet eyes on him and said, "What is an arm? You have another."

And so I suppose that began their courtship. How many, I wondered, began that way, in the wake of war? How many like Noah reached out with the only hands they had left to women who would help them heal?

We were getting north now, and the humpbacked hills had lost all their reds and yellows. Gaunt winter was on the way. At the Carbondale depot we collected Delphine's trunks and paid a man with our last money to take us home.

Noah felt every jolt in the road. We seemed to make no headway whatever, after the speed of the train. But one last rise and there it was—the great, gray river rolling past Tower Rock on the Missouri side. Down the last dip was the scatter of houses around the landing, and the house astride the Devil's Backbone, halfway up. The leaves were off the trees now, so we saw the smoke from our chimney.

The sight of it sent the blood hurrying through my veins. I'd been sent to bring my brother home, and here he was. So that was the very last time when I was truly young, young in my heart. That breathless moment in the rattling backboard, almost safely home.

How empty Grand Tower seemed, after the boom of Cairo. There was emptiness to our house too, a vacant, staring look about the windows. But then the kitchen door flew open, and out plunged Cass, down the porch stairs, pounding to us before we could get the trunks down.

My arms were out to her. But it was the old Cass before Calinda—whey-faced and wan. Her dress ought to be tight on her, but she was lost in it. Her eyes were big and haunted in their former way.

She flung herself at me, and there up on the porch Calinda was standing. She wore a black tignon. Evening was coming now, and there was evening in her face.

"Mon Dieu," Delphine murmured, "what has happen?"

Cass had come out without her shawl. She trembled against me like a broken bird, then turned to Noah. Her eyes filled when she saw his pinned-up sleeve. She grabbed at her own arm because she'd known he'd lose his. She'd suffered its loss in her visions. She'd felt the doctor's cleaving knife through more nights than I knew, there on the windowsill.

She took his hand and mine in a somehow formal way. From the porch Calinda gestured Delphine to her. And so it was only the three of us, my brother, my sister, and me, walking now around the house, above the chicken yard. We were making for the woodshed, dreaded through the summers because of the snakes.

Cass threw open its sagging door. I staggered against Noah. Inside on two sawhorses was a coffin. A plain wood coffin nailed down.

A terrible howl began low in me. "Mama!"

"No!" Cass said. "Paw."

I couldn't think. Something lay on the coffin lid within the shadows of the shed. Noah went in there and brought it out—a gray forage cap and the buckle off a belt with some insignia on it, something military. I wouldn't have known what it meant.

But Noah could read it clear. "He was in Polk's army. He took up with the Secesh side. I fought against him and didn't know." There was wonder in Noah's voice, and this was the first time he'd spoken of the battle.

"We drove 'em back through the woods, past their camp. I'd lost my musket by then. It never would fire. When we fell to looting the camp, Grant made us torch the place to learn us not to steal. The smoke drew Polk's fire from across on the Kentucky side. That's when I lost this." He touched his sleeve.

All I could think was that they'd ship a dead man home, even a dead reb. But they'd let a one-armed boy find his own way.

I wouldn't mourn Paw. He'd learned us long before how to get by without him. And all he'd left behind himself was there in Noah's hand. It was fitting that Paw had ended up fighting on the other side. He'd never been on ours.

"They brought him back by boat," Cass said. "They put the coffin ashore and sent word up from the landing."

How dark the hollows under her eyes, like bruises. She looked deep at our brother. "Noah, Mama thought it was you, come home in the coffin. She thought it was you she'd lost."

Cass seemed to shrink. There was fear of us in her eyes.

"Cass, where's Mama now?" I said.

"Gone in the river." Her voice was low and lost. "Before we could stop her."

Gone in the river, when I'd been a daughter to her and done her bidding and brought my brother home.

He gathered us up in the arm he had left, and the three of us turned back to the house.

Time and the Mississippi River

Chapter Fifteen

It was that summer of 1916 when my dad took me and my little brothers down home to see his folks. Time has a different shape in Grand Tower, Illinois, and so when we got there, Dad was "young Bill," and we were young Bill's boys.

Summer afternoons are longer in Southern Illinois than anywhere else, and hotter. The sun hangs eternally just off-center in the blinding sky. Dad spent the afternoons mostly up in Great-aunt Delphine's room. He sat at her bedside by the window that looks out across the river to where the wedding party drowned long ago.

As one afternoon folded into the next, I began to see this was another reason for our visit. His aunt Delphine was dying.

Would she become another Grand Tower haunt, like the ghost woman with the flying gray hair who darted across the road and into the Mississippi? Like that ghost who grieved the loss of a son, though he was still alive?

My little brothers, Raymond and Earl, trailed Great-uncle Noah on all his afternoon chores. They'd never seen a one-armed man before. And this one could do what other people needed both hands for. He could peel an apple, kill a rat, bait a hook—all kinds of things deeply interesting to five-year-old boys. They had no idea he was entertaining them. They thought he was just going about his business.

The only one of us who napped was old Dr. Hutchings. He sat in his porch rocker, transparent with age, courteous even in drooping sleep. He had the dignity I saw in my dad. His clean white hands were folded neatly in his lap. These were the hands that had amputated Noah's arm in the first year of the war, after the Battle of Belmont. And how many more arms and legs, how many thousands, through all the blood-slick years of war?

I knew the story because Grandma Tilly told me. She was a talker when she got going, and could bring it all back for you. I saw for myself the amputated arm sinking in the churning river as they brought the wounded back to Cairo. I still see it.

Neither age nor the weather slowed Grandma Tilly. She was a whirlwind from early morning on, cooking and baking for extra mouths. She was up and down the stairs, fetching and carrying for Aunt Delphine, and not letting anyone else do it. Carrying her slops too because there was no plumbing in the house.

But she found a corner of every afternoon to round me up and lead me to the crest of the Devil's Backbone, to a flat rock they called the devil's footstool, just among themselves. It had aeroplane views out over the river and Tower Rock. There we sat, both of us barefoot, while she brought back the old times for me. She handed over the past like a parcel, seizing these days to do it.

She couldn't sit there idle, of course. She didn't know how to be idle. She brought an old sewing basket with pearls and little shells on the lid, and her mending. She darned over a milkglass egg and spun out her yarns.

At first I didn't know how to listen to tales that old. But we began to edge across the years toward each other, Grandma Tilly and I. I began to see the yellow lamplight on their faces, just a flicker at first. I heard calliope music wavering over the water.

At every turn the story took, I remembered I was just about the age now they were then. Except for Cass. She was younger.

"What happened to Cass?"

"She's down there." Grandma Tilly pointed a bent finger to a long dip between the Backbone and another outcropping called Oven Rock. It looked like overgrown wilderness. "It was a graveyard, but they didn't keep it up."

By then I knew how she worked to keep the sentiment out of her voice. Still, it was about to break through.

"She died young?"

"She died the year after the war. 1866. She was seventeen. Dr. Hutchings called it diphtheria." She always spoke of him as Dr. Hutchings. She addressed him as Dr. Hutchings.

"If it hadn't been diphtheria, it would have been something else. I washed her poor bird-body and dressed her in the sprigged dimity she'd worn that night to the showboat. I put her in her coffin and wouldn't let nobody near her. I held her in my arms one last time, and then I let her go again. She give up on life after Calinda left us."

I waited for more and then said, "Why did Calinda leave?"

"Well, she was too dark to stay, wasn't she? She couldn't pass. I always thought she was the color of honey at the bottom of the jar. I expect she thought people would put two and two together, and it would give Delphine away. You know how there was always rumors about them.

"No, she had it in her mind to go out to California. She said out there she'd be light enough to be Spanish. And she was good with money. She always had some put by, for the journey. She was a true bird of passage, always ready to take flight."

Grandma Tilly looked out across the river, to the west. "A hard journey in them days, before there was a train to take you all the way to California. We knew she'd go, and I was scared Cass would go with her. I though the trip might kill her. But of course staying behind is what finally done her in.

"Calinda was what they call a conjure woman, down yonder in New Orleans. She could tell your fortune, you know, and there'd have been a market for that in the more built-up areas. Cass had the gift too. It's what drawed them together, closer than sisters. But I suppose it was too late for Cass. I think she'd been wore out by her visions before Calinda come among us."

A hot breeze stirred the trees.

"We never heard tell of Calinda again. I expect she prospered. She had all those talents, didn't she? But we never heard. They had a brother too, remember. In Paris, France. But they were the free people of color. And after the war they had to find new selves. I suppose it was just better to cut their ties and go it alone. Think how many more there must be like them—perched very quiet up on people's family trees. Safe now from being called ugly names."

That was the last afternoon of our visit. It had taken Grandma Tilly the week to tell her story. She bit off a thread—she didn't have all her teeth, not nearly all. Then she stole another look at where the graveyard had been. Down where Cass was.

"And your paw," I said. "He's down there?"

"Yes, he's down there. We didn't bury Cass next to him. There wasn't any point to that. And of course Mama's not there." Grandma Tilly turned away from me. "Mama went in the river."

It was time to leave then, and somehow I wasn't ready. We climbed up off our rock, the devil's footstool, for the last time. Grandma Tilly had to look way up at me. I was getting to be what she called a big, tall galoot. We started down the Backbone to the house.

"They never did get married, you know," she said, almost offhand. "You're old enough to hear it."

"Who didn't?"

"Delphine and Noah."

"They never got married? But—"

"Oh, we put it around that they were married. We said they went up to Centralia or somewhere to tie the knot. I forget now where we said they went. But they never did. It liked to break Noah's heart. But Delphine wouldn't have it. She said her kind didn't marry white men. And she was passing for white! She said it would betray all her traditions, said her mother—her *maman*—would turn over in her grave. Her mother died during the war, when New Orleans was occupied by our troops. We got that word.

"But anyway, Delphine never would marry Noah, though they're more married than most. But you know how she is. If she makes up her mind to something, or lapses into the French language, you just as well get out of her road. She'd make a mule look agreeable."

I remember one more thing Grandma Tilly told me. She said that time was like the Mississippi River. It only flows in one direction. She meant you could never go back. But of course we had. She'd taken me back.

We went on down to the house. She had a way of telling you so much, you thought you'd heard it all. And I knew where she'd learned that.

The night before we left Grand Tower, Great-uncle Noah wrung the neck off a fat fryer, to my little brothers' great excitement. Grandma Tilly fried it in batter for our picnic hamper. She loaded us down with deviled eggs and buttermilk biscuits. She piled us high with jars of her rhubarb preserves and looked around and around herself to see what else we ought to have.

We filled our bottles from their well. Dad personally filed down the points on the spark plugs, and we made an early start the next day. The three old folks were on the porch to see us go. We'd said our good-byes to Great-aunt Delphine the night before, up in her cluttered room under the portrait of her yellow-haired father. She couldn't speak, but those great fringed violet eyes ate us alive. The touch of her little pillowed hand lingered on mine long after.

We left in the cool of the morning. Being parked on the Backbone helped because the Ford started better on a slant. I got the engine to catch after no more than five minutes. We'd settled the little boys, brown as berries now, on the backseat. Then, in this miraculous morning, Dad climbed up into the heaving car on the passenger's side. He was letting me drive. My heart sang.

I was to drive, and let out the brake, and fiddle with the gas lever, so that Dad could turn back and wave to them up on the porch. He waved until the house and then the hill and then the town were swallowed in our dust.

We made good time going home, keeping the river on our left, retracing our route, though we had more flats. Raymond and Earl wanted to stop the night and make our camp where we had before. They wanted this trip to have an exact shape.

Dad pretty well convinced them that we'd found our original campground when it was time to pull off that evening, though we never found a trace of the old campfire. We built another one, and ate better that night than wienies on sticks.

After the dust of the day, there were circles around our eyes where the goggles had been. The twins were nodding off against each other before the dying fire. I sat next to Dad on the running board.

As if he'd waited for this moment, he said, "I've been thinking of getting into the war, if the country does." It shook me. Then I saw this was another reason for the trip.

"You'll think I'm too old for a soldier," he said, "and maybe I am. But they'll need doctors. I didn't want to spring it on you at the last minute. You'd have to take over at home till I got back, be there for your mother and the boys."

In the quiet, I heard my dad waiting. He wanted it to be

all right with me. He wanted my approval. Nothing this grown-up had happened to me before. This was something Grandma Tilly couldn't understand—how war promises a boy it can make a man out of him.

"Well, your dad went to the war, didn't he?" I said.

"Yes, he did."

"They can't fight a war without doc—"

"My father isn't Dr. Hutchings," Dad said. "Noah's my father."

I grabbed hold of the running board. The night revolved around me.

"And Delphine's my mother. She's slipping away, and I wanted this time with her. We couldn't be mother and son, you see. She didn't trust the world. She didn't trust the town. She never knew when somebody would . . . see her for who she was and turn on her. She wouldn't hand that on to me. It could have closed too many doors in my face. So I was named for Dr. William Hutchings. They had no other children, the doctor and your grandma Tilly, none of their own, so I was their son too. As you said, I had four parents."

He didn't mention love. It wasn't a word they used. But there was plenty they didn't mention.

"I'm proud of every drop of blood in me," Dad said, quiet to keep from waking the boys. "One day when you've had time to think it over, I hope you'll be proud too."

I remembered Grandma Tilly speaking of the blood hurrying through her veins. Now I felt the blood hurry through mine, flowing like the Mississippi River, as my dad and I sat there on the running board under a sky crowded with stars.

I didn't have to think it over. I was proud of anything that made me his son. I was proud of being Noah's grandson. And Delphine's grandson. I was older now too, a lot older than when this trip began, older and looking ahead. One day I'd tell a son of my own this story of who we were. A son, or a daughter with enormous violet eyes.

A Note on the Story

Researching the Civil War is enough to swamp any novelist's boat. That war remains the pivot on which all American history turns. It ground on for four endless years, raging on a thousand fronts. I could have spent the rest of my life researching that time. People do. But I had to carve out a place for my young characters to stand.

Because it's a story of two mysterious young women who come north from New Orleans, the focus of the story is upon the war on the Mississippi River. Since they needed a northern destination, I borrowed the hometown of my friend Richard Hughes, because all my stories are set in real places.

"Egyptians," as Southern Illinoisans still call themselves, were deeply divided, though mainly Southern in their sympathies in the first spring of the war. Raising enough Egyptian men and boys to form two Illinois infantry regiments, the Twenty-ninth and the Thirty-first, was the great achievement of John A. "Black Jack" Logan. His speeches repeated the battle cry, "The Union must be preserved, join the army and save the nation," never mentioning slavery or emancipation. He referred mildly to those like Curry Marshall who went south to join the rebel forces as "misguided boys."

The story of Noah's soldiering follows the history of that first year of war. The initial engagement on the Mississippi was the Battle of Belmont, meant to win the river and cut the Confederacy in two. U. S. Grant conducted it from his command post at Cairo (pronounced then and now as "Kay-row").

Nobody, including me, has ever had a positive word to say about Cairo, Illinois. Charles Dickens had been appalled by it on a visit before the war. It figures in the darkest moment of Mark Twain's *The Adventures of Huckleberry Finn* when Huck and Jim float past the town in the night and are swallowed by the slave-owning South.

But it was thought to be strategically located for the Union's grip on the river. At the time, it was the great metropolis of Southern Illinois with a population of twenty-four hundred—the largest city Tilly ever saw and a great factor in her decision never to leave home again.

The Battle of Belmont, Missouri, was only a skirmish, though costly, and it left the Southern forces in control. It could have stood for every battle ever fought in every war ever waged in that neither side really won. On the following day, November 8, 1861, the *Chicago Tribune* called it a "bad defeat" for the North. But it revised the reputation of U. S. Grant and gave him his first experience of command. By the following April, Delphine's beloved New Orleans was in the hands of Union troops.

A soldier's war is over on the day he loses a limb, and so Noah's Civil War lasted only weeks, not years. Like soldiers down the ages, he had to find his own way home, and a way to his future.

But what of those two young women who waft up the river from New Orleans in a scented cloud of mystery?

When Delphine says that her free people of color lived on a kind of island, lapped by a sea of slavery, she doesn't overstate the case. From the city's eighteenth-century beginnings, first as a French colony and then a Spanish colony, a society of free people of color, mainly people of mixed race, formed the beating heart of New Orleans.

Elsewhere in America and the Caribbean were black people who had won or paid for their freedom. But in New Orleans they founded a community that gathered economic clout and considerable—though precarious—social prominence . . . and inspiration for writers.

New Orleans hardly existed before 1718, but as early as

1724, the French issued *Le Code Noir,* the Black Code, an attempt to define and control a free black local populace. They were to have all the rights of any citizen with three crucial exceptions: They couldn't vote, hold public office, or marry a member of the white race.

The *gens de couleur* were even then developing into the artisan and mercantile class of the city. Having arrived early, many of them owned prime real estate. Theirs became an urban society that adopted and adapted the ways of their white neighbors. They were family-centered and Roman Catholic, and continued speaking French throughout the forty years of Spanish occupation—and a century beyond that.

By the time of Spain's rule, the free women of color had developed such a reputation for style, glamour, and disrespect for authority that the governor, Don Estaban Miro, issued in 1786 the most futile of all laws.

He forbade free women of color to wear hats. Since decency and etiquette dictated that a woman had to wear something on her head, the free women of color adapted the kerchiefs—"tignons" in New Orleans French—worn by slave women. But on the heads of the free women of color these tignons were apt to flaunt feathers and drip with precious gems. The "tignon" law lapsed at the end of Spanish rule, but in the American century that followed, the tignon lingered on as both a symbol of racial pride and a reminder of prejudice.

After the Louisiana Purchase of 1803, New Orleans

found itself a part of the United States, and ruled by Americans—often Southerners—who showed less tolerance than the Spanish and French. They were shocked at the amount of property owned by free people of color, and most of the owners were single women.

The custom of *plaçage,* of white men fathering families with their mistresses who were free women of color, shook the American newcomers to their shoes. How this arrangement began is shrouded in history and mystery. It may have come from the Caribbean, where women of color were often the mistresses of Spanish or French colonials, then encouraged in early New Orleans by the scarcity of European women.

Not every free woman of color became the mistress of a white man she couldn't legally marry. Those who did enter into this became famous as "quadroons," an elastic term that came to refer specifically to those mixed-race mistresses.

Their ranks were increased at the time of the Louisiana Purchase when free black people fled the slave uprising in Santo Domingo, the French colony that became independent Haiti. A number of these women, who were known in story and song as the "sirens," were renowned for their beauty.

The journalist Lafcadio Hearn described them in trembling prose: "Uncommonly tall were these famous beauties—citrine-hued, elegant of stature as palmettos. . . . Never organized to enter the iron struggle for life unassisted and unprotracted, they vanished forever with the social system that made them a place apart."[1]

But only the outcome of the Civil War erased them. The system of *plaçage* flourished through the American nineteenth century in New Orleans. The American regime that imposed new strictures on the free people of color—curfews and identity cards—was silent on the subject.

The loss of the Civil War destroyed New Orleans's economy. President Lincoln's Emancipation Proclamation of 1863 gave the free people of color a crisis of identity, since they were themselves often slave owners.

Most stayed on in New Orleans to rebuild. The system of *plaçage,* hardly mentioned in polite society, went further underground and was largely eliminated by the financial disaster of the war.

An unknown number of the women and girls who had been the quadroons—daughters and granddaughters of the sirens—went north if they could pass for white. Others who appeared Spanish were said to have gone to California. Some went to Mexico. They vanished from view to live among strangers, silent about their origins—leaving writers to imagine their fates.

[1] *Creole Sketches,* 1904.

Acknowledgments

I am grateful to Eordonna D'Andrea
for helping me find Calinda's song,

to Berthe and Jimmy Amoss of New Orleans

and

Patsy and Ron Perritt of Baton Rouge
for shelter and hospitality,

to Susan Overstreet Stevens
for direction,

and to Richard Hughes
for his hometown, Grand Tower.